THE EDEN MISSION

The Robinswood Press

First edition published 1995

Anthony Wall has asserted his rights under the Copyright, Designs and Patents Act, 1988 to be identified as the author of this work.

©Anthony Wall 1995

Printed and bound in Great Britain by Biddles Ltd., Guildford.

Stourbridge England

ISBN 1 869981 52 9

Supporting Environmental Awareness

The Robinswood Press will donate 20p from the proceeds of each copy of this book to the David Bellamy Appeal for the Solar Study Centre for environmental education at the Centre for Alternative Technology, Machynlleth, Wales.

Details of the Solar Study Centre are given on page 175.

For my dear seer, Vicky

'If all the beasts were gone, men would die from great loneliness of spirit. For whatever happens to the beasts soon happens to man. All things are connected...The earth does not belong to man: man belongs to the earth. All things are connected like the blood which unites one family...Whatever befalls the earth befalls the sons of the earth. Man did not weave the web of life: he is merely a strand in it. Whatever he does to the web, he does to himself.'

Red Indian Chief Seathl in a letter to Franklin Pierce,
President of the United States, 1855

Journalist and writer Anthony Wall has travelled widely to pursue interests such as natural history, art and the sea. His articles have appeared in many newspapers and magazines, and he has broadcast on both BBC and independent radio. He has written poetry for the Edinburgh Festival, documentary film commentaries, and has contributed to a highly praised *Reader's Digest* anthology on Antarctica. His other books are *The Anchor Trick* (Everest, 1977); *Sea Mysteries* (Piccolo, 1980); *Collision* (Collins,1985); *Dominic Dormouse Goes to Town* (Romer, 1993). He is married and lives in London.

Acknowledgements

I am indebted to Curt Maflin for his constant encouragement during the writing of this book.

My research for *The Eden Mission* was greatly aided by many generous experts. Space permits me to name only a few. They are Professor Ghillean Prance, Director of the Royal Botanic Gardens, Kew; Jonathan Shanklin, of the British Antarctic Survey; Dr. Bernard Stonehouse, of the Scott Polar Research Institute; Tim Inskipp, of the World Conservation Monitoring Centre; Amanda Hillier, of the Fauna and Flora Preservation Society; Carol McKenna, of Respect for Animals; marine engineer Keith Norledge.

I must also acknowledge invaluable help from staff of the following: the World Wide Fund for Nature, Greenpeace, Friends of the Earth, the Environmental Investigation Agency, BirdLife International, BBC Bristol, the Natural History Museum, the Geological Museum, the Meteorological Office, the Foreign and Commonwealth Office, the University of East Anglia, the American Cetacean Society, the Florida Department of Commerce, and Orlando's Sea World.

Foreword

The world - and it's the only one we've got - is in a terrible mess from misuse and neglect. Eco-terrorists and vested interests abound, polluting rivers, lakes and seas, draining wetlands, destroying ancient forests and trading in endangered species.

The Eden Mission, though a work of fiction, brings the real live world of conservation and the fight to save the planet to a whole new audience.

It also proves that it is not too late for us all to do our bit to save the Earth.

David Bellamy
The Conservation Foundation

Preface

Not so long ago, the term 'greenhouse effect' meant little to most people. Something to do with gardening...? How different now! Now that the environment is a matter of major concern, now that we are becoming ecologically educated.

But how much has changed, really changed, in recent years? Certainly politicians and scientists have made a start on trying to curb the worst abuses to our world. And, happily, some of those mentioned in my novel are declining. Others, though, are on the increase. So, far from being able to relax, conservationists are busier than ever.

Underlying all this are enormous problems: the widening gap between rich and poor, the fact that three-quarters of global resources are consumed by one-quarter of the population, the arrival each second of three new mouths to feed.

What of the solutions? Perhaps the main hope, idealistic though it may seem, is that humanity will see sense. The Earth, not money, is the only true wealth. It's our *collective* home to be shared with our fellows and fellow creatures.

Maybe the rich must become poorer, accept a lowering of their material standards, so that the poor can become richer. Maybe the technology that helped get us into this mess cannot get us out, and humankind will have to return to a simpler way of life. Maybe...

What do you think? What you think matters - yours is the generation that will need to be wiser and more responsible than previous generations. In your hands may rest the fate of the whole planet.

Anthony Wall, 1995

The book's background details are as accurate and authentic as I can make them. But, here and there, I have 'played' with the facts for the sake of telling a dramatic story. For example, there is no Marine Mammal Center in Santa Barbara, though similar institutions do exist elsewhere. The ship *Sea Shepherd* is an invention, in no way linked to the conservation charity of that name or any of its vessels.

A.W.

Victims

Suddenly the grasses shivered, but there was no wind. Silence, stillness, then more movement and the sound of a soft, gargling growl. The tall stems parted...and a fiery face thrust forward. Orange and white and black-barred, it was a face to strike terror into man and beast, a face like a warrior's daubed with war paint. A hungry tigress on the prowl. As fast, as fierce, but bigger and more beautiful than her tan-coloured cousin the lioness.

The great striped cat, perfectly camouflaged, crouched and stared intently at the lake. Her pale yellow-green eyes did not blink. Out there, under the water, lay the body of a deer she had chased, caught and killed. But then she had been robbed of her prize. She intended to get it back.

An hour earlier, just before dawn, the tigress had stalked a group of sambur deer filing down from the hills to drink at the cool lake and munch the green feast of water lilies spread over the surface. For twenty minutes the tigress crept closer and closer, soundlessly placing one huge paw in front of the other. Then, when she was forty feet away, she tensed her haunches like springs and exploded into a bounding charge.

Tail erect, ears forward, she crashed through the reeds, splashed through the water. Deer darted to right and left in a frenzy of white spray. But one stag, blindly panicking, turned towards the tigress. A fatal mistake. With a flying leap she brought the deer down, breaking his neck in a single bite.

1

The stag weighed 500 pounds, the tigress only 350, yet she would wade to land with him. She hauled her prey shorewards.

Then it happened. The tigress felt a sudden tug. The sambur slipped from her jaws...and was dragged under water. Crocodile snouts nudged her heels. Wasting no time, she fled to the lake's edge - minus her meal.

Twice in the hour since then, she had paddled back to try to retrieve the deer, snarling and swatting the water. But on each occasion she had lost her nerve. Finally, with an echoing roar of fury and frustration, the tigress retreated to the high grass.

Now she watched and waited. She refused to surrender the hard-won meal, her first catch in many tries. The tigress was very hungry. But her three cubs, fidgeting beneath a saja tree, were hungrier.

Once, there had been four of them, born blind in a cave six months ago. They grew sleek and fat on their mother's milk until the day they were ready to venture out with her and start learning how to hunt for themselves. It was then that their father, a swaggering giant of 550 pounds, seized one of the cubs and devoured it behind a bush. He tried again - but the tigress was alert, and spat a challenge that froze him in his tracks. Though he outweighed her by 200 pounds, he knew she would fight to the death to defend her young. The tiger had backed down and slunk off.

Turning from the lake, the tigress checked that the three cubs were safe before resuming her long vigil. The sun was high and hot, and she panted heavily. All around could be heard the buzz, hum, click, fizz and rattle of insects.

Ranee, as she was known by the wardens of this Indian nature reserve, was a splendid specimen. Nearly nine feet long, seven years old, in her prime. She should live to the age of eleven, maybe twice that. For the next seventeen months she would devote herself to rearing and teaching the cubs. The wardens could easily recognise Ranee by the stripes and squiggles on her cheeks and eyebrows - as distinctive as human fingerprints - quite different from those of her massive mate and the five other tigresses in his scattered harem.

By now the temperature had soared to 110 degrees Fahrenheit in the shade. Ranee still watched and waited. A snake slithered past her paw. She recoiled slightly, remembering a painful incident as a cub, but the snake trickled away through a crack in the ground and was gone.

In the late afternoon Ranee's patience was rewarded. The sambur buck floated to the surface. But it was surrounded by crocodiles - their teeth, ideal for gripping, could not tear off the firm flesh. Ranee glared, summoning her courage. The deer's body beckoned, fifty yards from the rim of the lake.

Quivering with anticipation, Ranee dashed forward. She swam strongly, ignoring the crocodiles, grabbed the sambur by the throat and began her return journey. Their two heads bobbed up and down between the water lilies. At last Ranee landed her catch. Laboriously she hauled the deer towards her cubs.

Crack!

Three small striped faces grimaced in alarm.

The bullet from the high-powered rifle entered through Ranee's right eye, ploughed on and shattered her brain. She moaned once, then collapsed over the body of the sambur. Suddenly she was devoid of grace and strength, her life switched off like an electric current.

The poacher lowered his gun. A pity to spoil the pelt with a second shot. He'd wait until he was sure the big cat was dead. But not too long - the wardens might catch him. Still, it was worth the risk when a tiger-skin coat could fetch £63,000 in a Tokyo shop.

That same day, eight thousand miles away, another armed man was preparing to pursue his quarry. He was perched on a boat's seesawing bow. Cursing the cold, he stared ahead at the sullen blue-black swell of the Southern Ocean. Sooner or later he would spot what he was looking for - a tell-tale spout that signalled the coming battle. Then there would be no time to feel cold, no time to feel at all. Meanwhile he should give thanks that he wasn't on the Antarctic mainland, where the temperature had been known to fall as low as minus 130 degrees Fahrenheit.

Far to starboard an iceberg loomed. Miles long, a hundred feet high, glittering like a gigantic diamond. The man still scanned the horizon. To help him locate his target, the boat had echo-sounders and a look-out up on the masthead, but the man trusted his own eyes and instincts more than anything else.

On a nearby ice-floe thousands of Adelie penguins, like spectators, stood in rows.

A shout came from the look-out. Already the gunner below was manoeuvring the harpoon cannon into position, his attention focused on the slanting jets that rose from the sea half a mile ahead. The whale had just surfaced and was spouting, at fifteen-second intervals, before taking breath for another deep dive.

With engines racing, the catcher boat closed in...800 yards, 400, 200. The gunner licked his lips. One good clean shot should do it. He looked down on the enormous wrinkled body, took aim - behind the head - and fired. A loud report was followed by a whine of running rope as the six-foot, 160-pound steel harpoon arrowed through the air at sixty miles an hour. It hit home with terrific force. The tip exploded deep inside the creature, sending out barbs. Threshing its tail flukes, the whale began an ordeal of panic and pain.

The gunner surveyed the red streamers trailing from his tethered victim. It would die soon enough.

But not everyone who witnessed the gory spectacle remained as unmoved as the harpoonist. The medical officer, watching from the factory ship where the carcass would eventually be processed, felt shame and disgust. A sperm whale, he noted, adjusting his binoculars. Officially protected by international agreement. That didn't stop these men. The whole business of whaling sickened him. As a doctor he was trained to save life, not take it, and he sympathised more with the whales than with the whalers whose health he was employed to safeguard.

The medical officer frowned, reflecting on what he knew about whales. Not fish but mammals: air-breathing, warm-blooded, bearing their young live, nourishing them on milk. A sperm whale had the heaviest brain of any animal - six times the weight of a human's. Did this mean high intelligence? Some scientists believed so. Certainly sperm whales were socially responsible creatures. When a calf was born, females would lift it to the surface for its first breath. They would guard the mother from attack during the birth, 'baby-sit' the youngster while she went diving for food, even suckle a strange calf. If a whale had a deformed jaw and couldn't catch prey, other whales would feed it.

Peering through his binoculars, the medical officer grimly observed that the harpooned sperm whale kept up its hopeless fight.

What a cruel waste! he thought. Science could learn so much from an amazing mammal like this. How was it able to dive two miles deep and stay under for as many hours? The pressure down there would crush a man beyond all recognition. How did the whale communicate over hundreds of miles? How did it use echoes to find its prey in the ocean gloom, to stun fish, diagnose illness in another whale? Questions - to which the answers could prove invaluable. But instead of learning, men threatened to wipe the species out.

Aboard the catcher boat no such thoughts crossed the gunner's mind. He was busy trying to solve a sixty-foot, sixty-ton problem: a sperm whale that refused to give up. The harpoon had not found the vital spot - the gunner blamed the choppy sea for spoiling his aim - and now the whale was towing the 110-ton boat behind it. Even with engines reversed, the craft kept moving forward. The gunner got ready to fire a second harpoon.

In the blood-stained water the mammoth beast continued its agonising struggle. He was a mature male, a bull. His slate-blue body bore scars, souvenirs of epic battles with giant squid he had hunted in the dark depths. The biggest of these pink monsters, whose human-like eyes were more than fifteen inches across, weighed 42 tons and measured 66 feet. But even their powerful beaks and ten suckered tentacles were no match for the whale's eight-inch teeth.

The gunner fired the second harpoon.

The whale gave a convulsive shudder. His life was nearly over. A life that had begun thirty years ago as a tiny calf in the sparkling Indian Ocean. At the age of five he had left his mother and joined other young males in a bachelor group. When his blubber thickened, he migrated to colder waters where food was more plentiful. At 25 he became master of a 'pod' of twelve cows which remained with their calves in tropical seas.

Although he was dwarfed by the hundred-foot blue whale, could not sing like the sweet-voiced humpback whale - both of which fed on plankton - his sort were the largest of the toothed whales, the same majestic breed as Moby Dick.

Each year he made the long journey back from the Antarctic to mate. But not this year. For three decades, the bull had eluded harpoons. Now he died, spouting thick blood.

The gunner nodded with satisfaction. Soon the vast corpse was winched alongside. Then, swinging slowly, the catcher boat chugged towards the factory ship whose stern gaped open like a mouth to swallow the whale. Once inside, it was hauled up a ramp.

The whale was efficiently disposed of. Its domed head yielded fifteen barrels of spermaceti oil for use in cosmetics; its body, oil for lubricants and leather softening; its belly, ambergris (the residue of squids' beaks) for perfume. Other products would later include crayons, candles, soap, pet food, fertiliser, glue. All these could be obtained from vegetable sources. But as long as unscrupulous people paid, whalers would go on breaking the law.

Sadly, as he saw the mighty animal disappear, the medical officer walked away. Behind him a helicopter lifted off with a swish and swirl of blades. Whale-spotting? He wondered, not for the first time, what was really happening aboard the factory ship. Whaling was bad enough - but he suspected something still more sinister. However, he had learned that it wasn't wise to ask too many questions round here.

In the Antarctic, you could vanish without trace.

Far, far to the north, off the coast of Norway, an oil-tanker crawled through fog. Usually the captain loathed such conditions. But today he was pleased - for the clammy cloud would conceal his activities. Leaning forward on the bridge, he gave orders to wash out the ship's tanks. Within minutes a sticky stinking stream of brown liquid was gurgling into the sea. Even when unloaded, a tanker retains about 2,000 tons of oil at the bottom of its tanks. That sludge has to be removed before a new cargo is taken on. Why pay to have the tanks cleaned in port if you could do it for nothing yourself? The captain's action was irresponsible, illegal and punishable with a heavy fine. But who can arrest an invisible culprit? He blessed the fog as the ship stole away from the scene of the crime.

Hours later a violent storm blew up, clearing the fog. Buffeted by wind, sea-birds sought refuge on the calmest water - which was those patches slicked with oil. Not long after, the first grease-caked casualties started to stagger ashore. Guillemots, gannets, puffins, razor-bills, little auks, kittiwakes. The final death toll would be fifty thousand.

News of the pollution spread fast. People gathered on the beaches, but they were unable to help the birds - except by putting them out of their misery. As a naturalist explained to a tearful woman onlooker, oil often blinded birds. It burnt their skin, stomachs and livers. It also removed the waterproofing from their feathers, which insulated them against cold and wet, so they couldn't float properly or catch fish. And if the birds weren't poisoned by swallowing oil after preening, they would probably die of pneumonia.

Singly or in small groups the bedraggled creatures stumbled to land. A three-foot gannet, normally brilliant white, pecked feverishly at its ruined plumage until a rifle-shot rang out.

By nightfall a two-ton pile of dead sea-birds had been collected on the shore. Someone set it ablaze. Sparks crackled amid whirling smoke. Excited, cherry-cheeked children ringed the bonfire; only the older ones understood that this was no celebration. For several nights to come there would be plenty of bodies to feed the flames.

Ninety miles inland, nothing broke the forest hush. A full moon silvered the treetops and light leaked down to the snow-covered floor beneath. Scraps of mist seemed caught on prickly branches.

From the shadows, a ghostly shape glided into a clearing. Two amber eyes searched the dappled darkness. Stealthily the wolf advanced. Hunger had driven him from his snug den. He knew where to find a good meal. Not the mice and birds he had lived on lately, but a hare he had killed and buried in the frozen ground to keep it fresh and safe from crows and ravens.

As the dog-wolf wound through the trees at an effortless lope, which could carry him as far as 120 miles in a single day, his thick brown-grey-yellow fur gleamed in the moonlight. He was a fine big dog: $5^1/_2$ feet from nose-tip to tail-tip, weighing a hundred pounds. In a pack he would have been leader. But there are no packs now - men had seen to that.

Wolves were regarded as enemies. Yet, like other predators, they performed a useful service by controlling the numbers of animals which destroyed farmers' crops. They made loyal pets if raised from cubs, and led a communal life that was a model of harmony and co-operation.

The wolf trotted on, nearing his food store. Strangely, since he was capable of detecting a smell from $1^1/_2$ miles and could hear loudish sounds more than four miles off, the wolf failed to notice a figure fifty yards away.

The man was half drunk, angry after a quarrel with his wife. He had stormed out of the house, taking a gun. He felt like shooting something. Suddenly the wolf appeared in front of him. The law said he must not pull the trigger. But he did - again and again. At that moment a cloud smothered the moon. The big dog dropped dead...leaving just four wolves alive in the whole of Norway.

8

Five thousand miles to the south-west, on the edge of Newfoundland, great glistening rafts of ice jigsawed the Atlantic. From above, each piece revealed a pattern of dark dots. Harp seals. Mothers and babies.

At birth the pups had seemed too small for their baggy yellow coats. But a diet of rich, mayonnaise-like milk soon filled them out. Then they had changed their fur - to a dense woolly white. Dazzling. In all nature there could be few prettier, more appealing sights. The pups were curious and trusting.

Now hunters came, wielding wooden clubs, battering the babies senseless. Plaintive cries reached their helpless mothers. The clubbing continued for weeks. This yearly slaughter of tens of thousands must be finished quickly - before the 'whitecoats' shed their beautiful fur. Sometimes, in the rush, pups were only wounded. They were skinned alive on the red ice.

The high price of unnecessary fur goods.

1 The Eden Mission

At the English port of Southampton it was raining, and had been for hours. A steady, soaking downpour. Water dripped from the dockside cranes; ran from the roofs of warehouses; washed the decks of liners, freighters, tugs and trawlers; spattered the windscreens of lurching launches. Seagulls sulked on the quay, or searched half-heartedly for food. The dingy sky showed no sign of brightening.

Not a day that promised excitement. Unless you happened to be young and about to set sail for faraway places and the adventure of a lifetime. Unless you were one of the lucky ones chosen to take part in The Eden Mission.

Sea Shepherd stirred at her moorings. The ship's steep side towered like a white wall above the clustering figures. A sailor peering down from the deck beheld a picture of marching mushrooms, as umbrellas formed into a line and began to advance. Now people were trooping up the gangway. Once on board they were conducted to a spacious, brightly lit lecture hall.

Wet umbrellas were put aside - and all thoughts of the weather. Parents, teenagers, teachers, ecologists and journalists settled in their seats. Press and TV cameramen took up position. Everyone's attention turned to the platform, still empty, at the end of the hall.

Elsewhere on the ship, bustling crew members made final preparations for a long voyage. Research vessel *Sea Shepherd*, a clean-cut 5,000-tonner, looked like a small cruise liner. But she was equipped to carry out a special task, a serious task. Her reinforced bow could carve through ice, her diving-bell and miniature submarines explore the underwater world, her laboratories analyse everything from sea snake venom to marine nuclear contamination.

In the lecture hall, fifteen-year-old Susan Jenkins shifted impatiently. *Why don't they get on with it?* Susan's eyes roamed the walls. A black-and-white panda chomped a bamboo shoot, a gorilla pounded his chest, a leopard lolled on a tree branch. There were other posters too. She smiled at her friend Gary, sitting beside her, then started to read the names on a banner above the platform: The World Wide Fund for Nature, Greenpeace, Friends of the Earth, The Fauna and Flora Preservation Society, The People's Trust for Endangered Species...

'Ladies and gentleman.'

At last!

The booming voice of Ben Bellingham, Britain's most famous naturalist. Susan stared in awe at the big burly man she had seen so often on television. His curly hair and beard were redder than she remembered.

'Sorry for the delay,' Bellingham went on. 'But at least it's given you a chance to dry off.'

There was a ripple of laughter in the audience.

'Right,' said Bellingham briskly, 'down to business, the reason you and I are here. The Eden Mission.'

Gary and Susan exchanged an amused look - they liked his no-nonsense approach.

The naturalist continued: ' For those of you who don't know, I'll outline the mission's aims. Then I'll explain why it's vitally important, and I'll also be talking about the young people who are joining in this conservation crusade.'

Susan felt a tingle run up her spine.

Bellingham strode across the platform to a huge colourful globe. He spun it vigorously and launched into his speech.

'Around the world, each day, at least fifty species of animal or plant disappear for ever. By the year 2000, it may be a hundred a

11

day. Some thirty per cent of all land is desert or semi-desert - the Sahara, for example, is spreading like an incoming tide - and more and more of the earth is crumbling to dust. The sea, which covers nearly three-quarters of our planet and on which we depend in countless ways, could become sterile.'

Pausing, he took a sip from the glass in front of him, then added: 'Who's to blame for all this? We are. Human beings. Greedy, ignorant, short-sighted humans. We're wrecking the world, robbing it, poisoning it, turning it into a rubbish dump. Unless we stop - and start respecting nature - there won't be much of a future for any of us...'

Bellingham came to halt, as though he had been interrupted. After a moment's hesitation he resumed: 'Er...sorry. This is sounding like a sermon. I'd better get off my soap-box.

'The Eden Mission is an international campaign,' he told his audience. 'An all-out effort to save the environment from further destruction. Throughout Europe, America, Africa, Asia, Australia, teams of conservationists - professionals and volunteers - are working in round-the-clock relays. They have a tremendous fight on their hands, an army of enemies. Oil and atomic pollution, acid rain, pesticides - now found even in Antarctic penguins - the mindless felling of rain forests, whaling, the illegal wildlife trade...'

A deep silence had fallen over the audience. Ben Bellingham concentrated on the rows of attentive faces. 'This is the most urgent project of our time. A matter, literally, of life and death. The Eden Mission must succeed.

'And *Sea Shepherd*'s role in the global operation? Crucial. The ship serves as an ocean-going headquarters - gathering data, via satellite, about the mission's many activities and acting as a link between the various task forces.'

Besides that, Bellingham explained, the experts aboard *Sea Shepherd* were conducting their own research and protection programme... 'a programme our younger passengers can help with.'

Gary caught Susan's eye and grinned.

'*Sea Shepherd* sails in an hour,' Ben announced. 'She'll be gone for a year. First stop Florida, then on to the Amazon, then Antarctica.'

He crossed the platform. 'Ladies and gentlemen, I want to show you some slides which illustrate why The Eden Mission cannot be allowed to fail. First, though, we'll take a short break...'

Susan's cheeks were flushed, Gary noticed. He felt it too - exhilaration. They'd soon be off!

The dark-haired boy, a few months older than his blonde friend, tended to make rather a point of appearing cool. Unlike Susan. Her blue eyes shone now as she enthused. The voyage, Ben Bellingham, the other teenagers travelling with them, the cabin where her luggage had already been stowed... it was all so exciting. Gary nodded eagerly, swept along by Susan's happy chatter.

A journalist in front of them mumbled to his colleague: 'Why's it called The Eden Mission anyway?' Susan, who had just finished a sentence, answered before she could check herself. 'Easy. After The Garden of Eden. The perfect place for people and animals and plants - living together.' The journalist didn't respond.

Suddenly the lights in the lecture hall dimmed. 'Your attention, please.' Bellingham again. Time for the slides. Up on the screen came a picture of a spotted ocelot fur coat, an elephant-ivory ornament, an ostrich-feather hat, a striped zebra rug, a crocodile-skin handbag and snake-skin shoes.

'A few of the frivolous luxuries we make from wild animals,' he commented.

The next slide showed a selection of poachers' weapons: rifles, machine-guns, poison arrows, wire snares. 'An arrow *can* kill an elephant in twelve hours - but sometimes death takes months. Poachers may even poison the beast's food with sulphuric acid from car batteries, causing slow and agonising torture. Wire snares often catch large antelope. If they do break free, the wire cuts into their flesh and they die later of infection.'

The screen went blank and a spotlight fell on Ben. 'We should all be ashamed of ourselves for letting this happen. More than a thousand animals - including leopards, gorillas and rhinos - face

13

the threat of extinction today because of human callousness. Not only do we slaughter our fellow creatures for pleasure and profit, we also destroy their habitat and capture them for zoos, the pet trade and vivisection...'

The spotlight faded and another picture appeared on screen. A rhinoceros.

One of fewer than 10,000 left alive, Bellingham reported. In 1970 there were 100,000. But ruthless hunting drastically reduced the population...and the carnage was continuing. Poachers killed rhinos for their horn. Some of it went to North Yemen to make dagger handles, the majority to East Asia to be ground into medicine. The Chinese believed that powdered horn cured colds, measles, nosebleeds, vomiting, heart weakness. The Japanese claimed it fought fever. Certain people even swore by it as a love potion.

'Most poachers are poor. So the temptation to earn money by any means, however risky, is very strong. They may work as farmers for £400 a year - less than they'd be paid for a single horn. A merchant will sell it to consumers for £95,000 and upwards.'

More slides followed.

A chimpanzee. Valued at £3,300 on the black market. Much in demand for bio-medical research, travelling acts, photography, tourist attractions and the television and film industries.

A hyacinth macaw. Going price £8,500 to an avid collector.

A peregrine falcon. Bought by Arab falconers for £1,000 each.

Seeing the peregrine, Gary forgot everything else. His favourite bird! It could stoop at over two hundred miles an hour, spot its prey more than five miles away. Peregrines had once nearly died out in Britain through eating pigeons which had fed on grain sprayed with pesticides...

Bellingham's voice broke into the boy's reverie. He was talking about Amazon dolphins. These gentle creatures, already threatened by pollution and river-damming schemes, were being killed - their eyeballs sold as ornaments and lucky charms in cities such as Rio de Janeiro.

Gary grunted disgustedly, and Susan's face showed *her* feelings.

The naturalist then mentioned another 'charming practice': eating bear paws. Considered a delicacy in Japan, Taiwan, Hong Kong and Singapore, the paws of hunted bears are imported from China.

'The wildlife trade is a worldwide business, worth billions of pounds. There are strict rules to control that trade. However, some countries don't agree to them. Others say they do, but allow crooks and cheats to get away with murder - animal murder. That's just one of the reasons why The Eden Mission is a top priority...'

Bellingham glanced quickly at his watch. 'I see time is running out. A few final words. *Sea Shepherd*'s programme includes trying to save grey whales and sea otters from oil pollution off California; manatees from being chopped up by speedboat propellers in Florida's waterways; Amazon dolphins from extermination. We have other tasks too, which I can't go into now. The six youngsters sailing with *Sea Shepherd*, all keen conservationists, will make a valuable contribution. But they'll also have to continue their school studies...'

Someone in the audience groaned.

Ben grinned broadly. 'Thank you for listening, ladies and gentlemen. Wish us luck!'

Loud applause. Then he answered last-minute questions from journalists. The audience - clad once more in raincoats, and clutching umbrellas - began to file out. Parents hugged their children, whom they wouldn't see again for twelve months, and gave good advice that would probably be forgotten or ignored. There were some tears.

Neither Gary's nor Susan's parents were present. They had already said their goodbyes at home and were glad to be spared emotional partings aboard *Sea Shepherd*.

By now the lecture hall was empty - except for six young people, eyeing each other somewhat warily, and the three teachers responsible for daily lessons.

Bellingham greeted them. 'Welcome to the team. I know we're going to get along fine...'

His next words were drowned by a sudden blast from *Sea*

15

Shepherd's horn. Almost imperceptibly the ship started to move. Ben's steady gaze rested on the group.

'Well... this is it.'

2 Shipmates

After the lecture, a tall, ferret-faced man had pushed people aside to be first down the gangway. He didn't look like someone much concerned with conservation. He wasn't. Sploshing through puddles, he hurried to a phone box on the quay. He dialled a number. His boss would find the report *very* interesting.

Waving parents watched *Sea Shepherd* glide away between lines of moored vessels, like a guard of honour. Her bright white hull shone luminously against sea and sky, both the same shade of grey. The teeming rain had stopped.

Leaning on the ship's rail, Susan was surprised by a twinge of sadness - she had nobody to wave to. Gary, sensing this, patted her on the back. Although they'd been friends for only three years, it often seemed they could read each other's minds.

Casually, so as not to draw attention to themselves, they turned sideways and observed their fellow passengers...to find that they themselves were being scrutinised. An attractive girl in expensive leisure clothes peeked back at Gary. Vanessa - he remembered the name from their brief meeting earlier. Sixteen years old; blonde, like Susan.

Her hair's dyed, I bet, Susan thought. She had already nicknamed the older girl *Vain*essa and decided she was a flirt.

Gary nodded, a little self-consciously, but Vanessa was now

studying the passing port scene - as though the ships hooting farewell were paying tribute to *her*.

Susan's eyes flitted rapidly over the other teenagers. All boys. Yves, good looking, half-French; Norman, solemn and bespectacled; and Darren, with the discontented face. Beyond them the three teachers talked earnestly. Planning lessons, guessed Susan.

Soon after, the passengers went below, leaving Gary and Susan alone on deck.

'They seem quite a nice lot,' said Gary cheerfully.

Susan made no comment, then: 'S'pose you've gone soft on that girl - what's-her-name...Vanessa? I saw you ogling her.'

Gary laughed. 'Rubbish. And you're a fine one to talk - don't pretend you aren't keen on Yves.'

Susan stuck out her tongue. 'Anyway, what do you care? You're not my guardian.'

He shrugged good-naturedly.

Susan was beginning to feel ashamed of her mean thoughts, and changed the subject. The Eden Mission, that's what really mattered. They both knew it. And if she hadn't won an ecology essay competition and a prize of places for two aboard *Sea Shepherd*, neither of them would be here.

She rested her hand on Gary's shoulder and looked at him cheekily. 'You may be a pain in the neck sometimes, but I'm glad you're coming with me.'

As Southampton slid astern, *Sea Shepherd* nosed into the thumping waters of the English Channel. At that moment the sun squinted through a crack in the cloud. On the horizon the sky's grey paint was peeling, revealing blue. A good omen?

Gary followed Susan down the companionway. 'See you at dinner,' he said, before entering the cabin he shared with Norman. As one of the girls, Susan had Vanessa for a room-mate. Next door were Yves and Darren.

Susan hesitated outside her cabin, fiddled with her cardigan, ran a comb through her hair. Then, head held high, she made her entrance. Vanessa wasn't there. Susan relaxed, smiling at herself.

18

The smile faded fast. She's taken the bottom bunk! I was here first. Susan stared, glared at the fancy nightdress laid out on the pillow. Did she have the nerve to move it? No, not quite.

Fuming, she started to unpack. Sweaters, T-shirts, jeans, shorts and a dress. She yanked open the wardrobe door. A row of eye-catching outfits hung neatly on hangers. 'Its like a fashion store,' Susan muttered, shoving the hangers aside to make space for her own clothes.

In the bathroom she opened the mirror-fronted cabinet on the wall. It was crammed with bottles and jars. Perfume, shampoo, creams... Susan slammed the cabinet shut and pulled a face in the glass.

Meanwhile Gary was trying to make friends with Norman. Hard work. Norman proved to be a very serious young man, much given to using long words. Must've swallowed a dictionary, Gary thought. But he kept up the conversation. Then the studious teenager produced a pack of cards and proceeded to do a series of conjuring tricks that made Gary gasp. Norman might be fun after all.

Checking her watch, Susan confirmed what her stomach was telling her - dinner-time. She left the cabin and saw Gary and Norman emerging farther down the corridor. Yves and Darren also appeared. Already it was clear that when food was involved the teenagers wouldn't find it too difficult to be punctual. But where was Vanessa? Susan glanced at Yves and Darren - Darren deliberately looked away. Gary introduced her to Norman, who blushed. They climbed the stairs.

Appetising smells wafted from the ship's galley. The five youngsters almost broke into a trot as they neared the dining-room. Suddenly the riddle of Vanessa solved itself; she was talking to a sun-tanned sailor. Susan sniffed. Yves mouthed the word 'Dinner' as they passed Vanessa, and she arrived in the dining-room soon after.

There were thirteen seats at the captain's table - Gary counted them. Isn't that supposed to be unlucky? He wasn't superstitious, but... Susan prodded him. 'Gary, sit by me, Norman on the other

19

side.' The boys grinned as Susan, the youngest of the three, bossed them about.

Vanessa grandly took her place opposite, between Yves and the uncommunicative Darren. At one end of the table, near Ben Bellingham, the trio of teachers huddled - Geoffrey Baggalley (Geography and History), Maude Mimpriss (English and French), Peter Stokes (Maths and Science). At the other end of the table the captain and two officers completed the party.

Ben Bellingham rose to his feet. His eyes twinkled as he started to address the young conservationists. 'Hello again. You know most of the people here, including your teachers.' He made a sweeping gesture in their direction. For some reason they reminded Susan of sheep - and she bit her lip to stop herself giggling.

'But,' Bellingham added, 'there's one very important person you haven't met...Captain James Alexander.'

A lean, distinguished-looking man with grey hair, kind but shrewd brown eyes and a firm jaw raised a hand in greeting.

Bellingham continued: 'Captain Alexander - Jim to his friends, which you will all become if you follow orders - is the master of *Sea Shepherd*. As far as everyone on board is concerned, he's Alexander the Great...his word is law.'

Captain Alexander laughed, then introduced the two men with him. They were First Officer Philip Grant and Radio Officer Leslie Curtis.

Bellingham sat down, reaching for the menu. 'I dunno about you lot, but I'm starving.'

Two white-coated stewards padded in and began to circulate around the table. Gary ordered mushroom soup, quiche and salad, and fruit salad for dessert. Susan asked for the same, except that she wanted mixed ice-cream. Vanessa dithered daintily over the menu, seeking Yves' advice. She also consulted Darren, whose only retort was 'Please yourself'.

Soon the six were tucking in as though they hadn't eaten for a week. When appetites were satisfied, the clatter gave way to chatter.

Dinner over, some of the youngsters were now looking round rather restlessly. Bellingham called for quiet, then said: 'Before you leave, a couple of points. Tomorrow's schedule is on the notice-board outside. Do read it. I don't know what time you usually go to bed, but I suggest you turn in early. We've got a heavy programme ahead - and this isn't a joy-ride.'

Catching sight of Darren's miserable countenance, the naturalist hastily added: 'It isn't a funeral either, so there's no reason why we shouldn't enjoy ourselves.

'Oh, and one more thing. If you have any questions, feel free to come and ask me. Sleep well, shipmates!'

Saying goodnight to the others, Gary and Susan slipped out of the dining-room. They paused at the notice-board, then went up on deck.

A simmering sun was just sinking into the sea. Gary strained forward, as if expecting to hear a hiss, and watched the waves which seemed to be on fire. Beside him Susan said nothing. Her eyes were drawn to the new moon, a hammock slung at an impossible angle between two clouds, and the first blooming of stars. Gulls mewed and snickered around the ship's stern. The lightest of breezes tiptoed across the water.

Gary took a deep breath. 'Beats being at home, eh?' Susan sighed in agreement, forgetting that sooner or later she always felt homesick.

'Damn!' Susan was scowling.

Gary stared. 'What's wrong?'

'Vainessa - I've got to put up with her in my cabin. For months and months and months.'

'It's *her* cabin too,' Gary pointed out.

'Whose side are you on, Gary Izzard?'

'Yours, of course. But Vanessa may not be crazy about sharing with you either.'

Susan pouted. 'Huh!'

Gary put his arm through hers. 'Anyway, count your blessings. Imagine being Yves - with doleful Darren as a room-mate.'

She giggled. 'Yeah...things could be worse. I suppose I'll survive.'

They went on talking for a little longer. When Gary mentioned the thirteen chairs at the captain's table, Susan snorted. 'Don't believe that stuff, do you?' He reddened slightly. 'No, I...I just...' She interrupted: 'I liked the captain and the first officer. Not so sure about the radio officer though...Leslie Curtis. Gave me the creeps. Dunno why.'

Gary shrugged. 'He seemed OK to me.'

Crossing the deck, they started down the companionway. 'Get some beauty sleep - you need it,' said Gary. He ducked. 'And good luck with Vanessa!'

Susan dawdled in the corridor. Then, straightening her back, she walked briskly to the door, turned the handle and stepped inside the cabin. It was empty but the sound of running water came from the bathroom. Susan glanced at the bottom bunk; yes, the nightdress was still there.

Vanessa emerged from the bathroom, a fluffy pink towel wrapped round her head. 'Hi.' She treated Susan to a brilliant smile.

Vanessa sat down decorously on the bunk and began to dry her hair. Susan stood, hands in pockets, uncertain what to say or do. She shuffled across the cabin and peered out of the porthole.

The silence lengthened. Susan felt more and more uncomfortable. At last, turning, she blurted: 'Um, Vanessa... About the bunks. You weren't here when I moved in, and I meant to leave my stuff on the bottom bunk. The thing is...would you mind changing?'

Susan waited, heart thumping.

Vanessa arched her carefully plucked eyebrows and said: 'Of course I don't mind. I only took this bunk so as not to disturb you if I came in late.'

Susan smiled. Maybe Vanessa *was* a natural blonde.

Tucked up in the bottom bunk, Susan lay awake. Her brain buzzed with the day's events. Such a lot. And the voyage was only just starting. She pictured Gary, who always made an effort to be fair.

22

He's probably right about that man Curtis. Why had she disliked the radio officer...?

Susan's eyelids drooped. She thought she heard the click of a cabin door. Yves or Darren going for a midnight stroll? Her curiosity stirred. Funny... Susan fell asleep

She woke to find herself bathed in a buttery light, pouring through the porthole. Drowsily she wondered what she would do today. Then she noticed the bunk above her - like a low narrow ceiling - and realised where she was. At sea! Bound for adventure!

Susan sat up, swung her legs sideways and stood stretching for a moment. No trace of sleepiness now. A series of purring snuffles rose from Vanessa's bunk. Susan chuckled. So glamour girls snored, did they?

Ten minutes later Susan was on deck. She shivered with pleasure. The sun-spangled water folded and unfolded to the far horizon. The Atlantic, unimaginably wide and deep. Not a sign of land anywhere. Nice to be alone...

'Hello, Susan. Sleep well?'

She frowned at Gary. 'Wish you wouldn't creep up on me like that.'

Norman, who had been hidden by Gary, stepped into view. 'Oh... Good Morning,' Susan said sweetly.

Norman peered over the ship's side. 'Sea's green,' he commented. 'That means it's murky with plants, rich feeding for fish. Blue water is poor in marine life.'

He took off his spectacles and began polishing them on a huge red handkerchief. Rather vaguely he added: 'And did you know that barnacles, like those clinging to the bottom of this ship, might prove valuable to man? Their adhesive properties are being investigated to see if they can be used in tooth fillings and to mend bone fractures.'

Susan stifled a yawn. 'Fascinating. By the way, Gary tells me you're an ace conjurer.'

Norman beamed.

Just then Yves joined them.

23

'No Darren?' queried Gary.

'No, he's still fast asleep in his bunk.'

'Best place for him,' muttered Susan. Immediately she felt guilty, and quickly went on : 'That reminds me, did either of you go out late last night? I'm sure I heard your cabin door.'

Yves shook his head. 'Not me. I couldn't wait to turn in. Dropped off straight away. But I can't answer for Darren. Hey, maybe he's a sleepwalker.'

Susan looked thoughtful, then laughed with the others.

They were half-way through breakfast before Vanessa put in an appearance and nearly finished when Darren, puffy-eyed and grumpier than ever, slouched into the dining-room. No one even tried to engage him in conversation.

At 9.15 the six youngsters filed into the lecture hall. Back to school! First lesson, French. Darren skulked at the rear - until Maude Mimpriss, in a voice like chalk on a blackboard, ordered him to sit behind a desk at the front. Susan, although not a fan of Darren's, stared coolly at the shrill teacher. Silly old...

Yves, who spoke and wrote French fluently, was naturally the star pupil. But Vanessa did well too.

When the English lesson came it was Susan's turn to shine. She warmed a little to Miss Mimpriss after her praise.

Peter Stokes, a dominoes fanatic, taught maths. Norman proved brilliant at the subject. A real genius, Gary thought admiringly.

Then geography and history master Geoffrey Baggalley took over. He had once been a physical training instructor - and it showed. As he talked, he walked up and down and waved his arms as if doing exercises. Mr. Baggalley caught Susan giggling, but Gary put him in a good mood again by answering all the geography questions correctly.

At lunch the unsupervised teenagers were rather noisy, cracking jokes about their teachers. It was harmless fun among new-found friends. Only Darren remained remote, cut off from the lively talk. Now and then Susan glanced in his direction. He seemed unhappy rather than disgruntled, and she felt sorry for him. Once, their eyes

24

met. Susan couldn't be sure, but she thought she saw a slight response before he looked down.

A quick breath of fresh air, then the youngsters returned to the lecture hall. Ben Bellingham was waiting for them.

'Please take your seats in the front row. OK, who cares about conservation? Hands up.'

Everybody reacted.

Bellingham pointed to Vanessa. 'Why?' he demanded. Vanessa opened her mouth in surprise. 'Er...'

The naturalist repeated his question, more gently. 'Why, Vanessa? Why should you care what happens in Africa, the Amazon, the Antarctic or anywhere else that isn't your home? What's it got to do with you?'

He nodded encouragingly. 'Well?'

Vanessa stuck out her chin. 'Animals have as much right to be on earth as we have. More - they were here first. And if we're the most intelligent creatures, the only ones that are moral, it's our duty to look after the environment. Besides, nobody owns the world. All living things are part of nature. So in a way nature owns us... '

Blushing, Vanessa tailed off. Without thinking, Susan started to clap.

Bellingham: 'Bravo! You convinced me - and at least one other person.' Now Susan went pink.

Walking along the row, Bellingham added: 'Anybody else want to speak up for conservation? Yes, Gary.'

'Well, Mr. Bellingham, I was just wondering about the Amazon. The way the trees are being cut down - fifty thousand acres a day. Don't half of all plant and animal species live there?'

The naturalist leaned towards him. 'Quite right. Oh, and call me Ben.'

Gary went on: 'I've read that a lot of industry, agriculture and medicine is based on jungle products - rubber, coffee, bananas, quinine and so on. Also that the Amazon is a botanical treasure-house we've barely begun to explore. It needs to be protected for everyone's sake. Another thing - people are upsetting the world

25

climate by felling those trees...'

Bellingham chipped in. 'Right again, Gary. But the situation is even worse than that, I'm afraid, as you'll see for yourselves on this trip.'

Norman put his hand up. 'No one has mentioned the gene pool. If the number of species keeps falling, the planet may not be able to evolve to meet changing conditions - and life could die out.'

Ben rubbed his chin. 'Certainly done your natural history homework, haven't you?'

He strode to the table behind him, on which stood a glass jar. Turning, he said: 'I think you and I agree conservation is worthwhile.'

There was a loud murmur of assent.

Bellingham picked up the jar, full of cloudy liquid. Something was floating in it. 'Know what this is?' He unscrewed the lid and, taking a pair of tweezers from his shirt pocket, fished out the mysterious object. 'Open your hand,' he said to Susan. She squealed as he dropped what he was holding into her palm. Slimy and spotted...frogs' legs!

'Won't hurt you,' he reassured her. 'Just the legs of some unlucky Indian bullfrog which didn't hop off in time to save itself.'

He retrieved the exhibit, passed it round, then put it back in the jar. 'The reason I have shown you this is to illustrate a story. A horror story.'

In Asia, each year, 250 million frogs are killed. For their legs. To make delicate snacks, eaten by spoilt customers in Europe and America.

Hunted at night with lamps, the frogs are collected from ponds and rice fields and taken away to be 'processed'. This involves immersing the frogs in salt water to numb them. Next they are sliced in two, the top halves thrown aside. The maimed frogs crawl off to die, many minutes later.

'Not very pleasant, is it? But that's not all.

'Frogs feed on insects, which spread fatal diseases and ruin crops. By killing the frogs, Asian villagers have brought on an insect population explosion. The result: catastrophe. What to do? Farmers bought pesticides to combat the menace. The pesticides cost more than the income from frogs' legs...'

Yves raised his hand.

'Just a minute,' said Ben. 'There's another episode to the story.'

The main pesticide is DDT - banned in Europe and America but sold to developing countries. Asian people were soon suffering from chemical poisoning. And, ironically, the contaminated crops are exported to Europe and America. Meanwhile the insects have grown immune to pesticides. So higher and higher doses are used, further endangering human health and wildlife - 'including those poor frogs'.

Ben Bellingham folded his arms and concluded: 'Greed, ignorance and failure to respect the balance of nature have caused a disaster. It will take years to put right. Roll on The Eden Mission!'

When the youngsters left they were curiously quiet. Ben had given them plenty to think about.

Half an hour after, Gary and Susan were strolling on deck. 'Fancy a dip?' he asked. 'Yeah!' They raced each other to their cabins and grabbed their bathing things.

Lolling in the ship's pool, Susan remembered how Gary had taught her to swim on holiday three years ago. She splashed him playfully. Later, dry and changed, they set out to explore *Sea Shepherd* thoroughly.

In one of the corridors they spotted Darren emerging from a door marked RADIO ROOM. He didn't see them. Suddenly Leslie Curtis, the radio officer, appeared in the doorway. He glowered at Gary and Susan. 'What are you doing here? This section's out of bounds to you kids.'

Gary, with an eye on the retreating back of Darren, started to protest. 'But...'

Then he felt a sharp pinch from Susan - and had the sense to shut up.

3 Enemies

The big black Mercedes, driven by a broad-shouldered chauffeur, slid like a shark through Hamburg's traffic. The driver was skilful - and ruthless. He forced other cars to give way.

From the back seat, his cigar-smoking passenger growled: 'How much longer?'

'Only five minutes, Herr Kruger.' The voice was meek, almost nervous.

'Well, put your foot down, man.' Kruger flicked cigar ash on to the floor.

Less than five minutes later the Mercedes drew up in front of a towering office block. The chauffeur hurried round and opened the passenger door.

'Wait here,' Kruger ordered. Carrying a document case, the immaculately dressed businessman strode into the entrance hall. A commissionaire, who had been reading a newspaper, sprang to attention.

'Good evening, sir.'

Kruger nodded curtly. 'Sixth floor.'

The commissionaire summoned the lift. When the chief of Anilux Trading told you to do something, you did it. Fast.

Riding up in the lift, the commissionaire stared at his shoes and said nothing. How he hated Kruger! A tyrant. Yet he had a beautiful young wife. Married him for his money, must have. Money. If I didn't need this lousy job I'd quit Anilux right now.

The lift arrived at the sixth floor. Without a word, Kruger hastened away. In an outer office a secretary stood up as he approached. 'Ah, Herr...'

Kruger cut in: 'Are they all here?'

'Yes, sir.'

'Very well, Fraulein. Send in some coffee.'

Maximilian Kruger entered the boardroom.

'Be seated, gentlemen.' He leaned forward in his chair at the head of the polished mahogany table and peered disdainfully at the anxious faces around him. Unzipping his document case, he pulled out a sheaf of papers and slapped them down on the table.

'Bad news. Reports that our business is being jeopardised - not by competitors but by interfering outsiders. No doubt you've heard of The Eden Mission...'

A knock at the door. The secretary brought in coffee. 'Leave it,' said Kruger. 'We'll serve ourselves.' The secretary crept out.

'As you know,' he continued, 'most of the company's trade in furs and wildlife products is not permitted by the law. And if we let those lunatic ecologists have their way, it could ruin everything.'

Kruger poured himself a cup of black coffee. Then he looked up. 'They've got to be stopped.'

Houston, Texas. In a penthouse apartment with a spectacular view of the city, a telephone rang...and rang. Uttering a swear-word, a woman in high heels teetered across the thick carpet towards the relentless ringing. She wore a fur coat, jewellery, and could have passed as a starlet.

'Yeah?' she drawled into the receiver. A pause. 'Hold on.'

Covering the mouthpiece, she yelled: 'Honey, call for you. German guy. Says it's urgent.'

A tanned, middle-aged man in a dinner-jacket appeared. The woman handed him the phone. 'Please be quick - we're late for the party already.'

Her husband raised the receiver. 'Art Benton speaking. That

you, Max...? Hi. What's the problem?'

Benton sat down, motioning his wife to get him a drink. Several minutes ticked by. Benton had drained the glass. He stretched and said: 'Take it easy, Max. The organization isn't gonna let a bunch of nature freaks louse things up. There's more at stake here than a few goddam animal skins. There's the entire global enterprise. Oil, timber, mining, property - and other interests we'd better not talk about over the phone...'

Benton listened to Kruger's comment, then added: 'This Eden Mission doesn't stand a hope in hell. The organization will take care of that.'

As the light aircraft began its descent, law officer Miguel Osuna took in a view he had seen a hundred times before. But each time was like the first. From 3,000 feet, the bright-green forest treetops reminded him of curly hair, parted by a straight red road that marched on and on and out of sight. Here and there parakeets, as common as sparrows, swirled colourfully. Near the road, water winked in the early morning sunlight. A river. *The* river, compared with which most other rivers were mere streams. The Amazon! Four thousand miles long, two hundred miles from bank to bank at its widest, fed by ten thousand tributaries. One-fifth of the world's fresh water flowing through a jungle bigger than Europe.

The plane dipped as it approached the uneven landing strip.

Law officer Osuna checked his revolver and concentrated on the assignment ahead.

Splutter-splutter...the aircraft dawdled to a stop. Osuna thanked the pilot. Jumping to the ground, he gave his colleague the thumbs up sign, then half ran to a waiting Jeep.

The engine responded immediately. Osuna spun the wheel and headed for an appointment with Carlos Mendoza, as nasty a piece of work as you were ever likely to meet. At this moment he was under arrest for killing jaguars, ocelots and margays and selling their spotted skins. A murderer, gun-runner and drug smuggler.

Osuna must take him into custody but clever lawyers, themselves as crooked as criminals, had always managed to save Mendoza's neck. Sometimes Osuna wondered whether it was worth trying to enforce the law.

On his left, like floating flower petals, a dazzle of butterflies danced. Red dust spurted from the Jeep's humming tyres. Osuna swerved. An armadillo scuttled across the road. This place belonged to the old jungle inhabitants, not to modern men and cars. Osuna had inherited a love of the natural world from his father and was passing it on to his own children. He found himself whistling, entranced by the forest's magic tune - whoops, howls, screeches, chirrups, twitters that rose and fell amid the unending green.

A gentle wind unravelled the last of the mist from the branches of tall trees, some soaring nearly 200 feet.

Suddenly darkness enveloped him. He looked up. His cheerful mood evaporated. High above, casting exaggerated shadows, vultures circled on eight-foot wings. Watchful scavengers, never far from the dead or those about to die.

His mind returned to Mendoza and the animal skins. The Amazon's pretty little ocelots and still smaller margays face possible extinction - a threat hunters repeatedly level at jaguars, the top cats here. Brawnier than leopards, swift, cunning, power-packed. One blow from a paw, so soft while stalking, could smash a man's skull, bring down an ox. A jaguar might attack any animal, however large, and drag it through dense undergrowth for a mile to share the feast with mate and cubs.

They're crafty fishermen, too. Sitting on a log, a jaguar taps the water lightly with his tail - a plop like the sound of falling fruit or insects. Expectant fish rise to the bait. A flash and slash of claws, and he has hooked a scaly snack.

It is also said that he can imitate the voices of almost all the forest creatures, luring them into a trap.

King Jaguar. You paid him respect. Men who hadn't, had died or been maimed. Some who survived tell of being paralysed with fear, nailed to the spot by the golden spikes of his eyes.

31

At night his reverberating roar, a coughing 'Uh-uh-uh-uh-uh', rings faster and faster, louder and louder up to a thunderous climax which fades into muted grunts. When the jaguar speaks, other beings tend to fall silent.

The Jeep sped on in the mounting heat. Miles to go before Osuna reached the makeshift wooden jail where Mendoza was held prisoner.

On the road in front he saw a mushrooming puff of red dust. A lorry swayed towards him. He heard the tinny blare of pop music and a jeering chorus of shouts. Miners? Lumberjacks? Probably drunk after an all-night binge in one of the local settlements.

Passing them, Osuna glanced at the driver and the other men in the lorry. All wore the same mindless expression. But why were they shouting insults?

Then he noticed a group of Amazon Indians standing dejectedly by the roadside. A man, woman and child, nearly naked. Thrown off their land, he guessed, by 'superior' white men. South American governments have insisted they need the money from timber, farming and mining. Trees are felled to make luxury furniture and paper; to clear space for cattle that will be turned into hamburgers; to open up the deposits of tin, iron, diamonds. In thirty years this whole vast primeval forest could be reduced to a bald wasteland.

Osuna knew what so-called civilised people had done to the Indians - and he felt ashamed. In Columbus's day there were nine million Amazonian Indians. Over the centuries they have been poisoned, bombed, shot and struck down by deliberately-introduced diseases against which they have no resistance. Now there are fewer than 200,000. Much of the remnant population has retreated to remote corners of the jungle or ended up in squalid city slums.

Osuna ground his teeth. He couldn't help comparing the Indians, dignified even in defeat, with the lorry-load of rowdy drunks. If either were savages, it wasn't the Indians. They are the only ones who understand the forest, treat it with respect, harvest its treasures wisely. They know the secrets of the plants that can be used for food and medicine. The rain forest is sacred to them. They believe it holds up the sky.

Beautiful, dangerous, mysterious. A hundred million years it has stood. Osuna's reverence was akin to the Indians'.

In there, steeped in a stagnant and steamy atmosphere, you imagined you had travelled back to the beginning of the world. In there live iguanas, like scaled-down prehistoric monsters; brash gangs of parrots; slow, upside-down sloths; grotesque vampire bats; tiny monkeys, three inches high, chirping like birds; frogs that can secrete enough poison to kill 2,000 people; spiders with leg-spans of more than ten inches; army ants advancing in foot-wide, mile-long columns, flanked by officers, eating everything in their path; twenty-stone tapirs which look part pig, part horse, part elephant. In there too flourish flowers of every shape, size and hue - such as orchids - and bamboos sprouting 65-foot leaves, and plants with marvellous medical properties. And the Amazon itself, mightiest of all rivers, is home to no less an exotic array of species. Thirty-foot snakes, electric eels that can shock the life out of you, three-foot lizards walking on water, sting-rays, massive alligators typified by stitched teeth until the jaws yawn and snap, dragonflies hovering on seven-inch wings, shoals of savage fish that are capable of stripping a body to the bone in minutes...

The Jeep lurched as it hit a pothole, jolting Osuna's thoughts back to his assignment. Not long now.

He double-checked the safety-catch on his revolver and patted the pocket which contained the warrant for Mendoza.

Shadows fell over Osuna again. More vultures. Despite the warmth, he shivered. The jail was in sight at last.

Slowing the Jeep, he drew up at the wooden shack. Seconds later a man in uniform led out the handcuffed prisoner. Osuna showed his papers, and the two law officers exchanged a few words. Then, with evident relief, the other officer handed over Mendoza. He looked every inch the villain he was, his brutal air emphasised by a scarred cheek and murderous eyes.

Saying nothing, Osuna guided his charge to the Jeep. He chained

Mendoza to a fixed metal bar beside the driver's seat - and began the return journey.

They were about four miles from the jail when Mendoza doubled up, clutching his stomach. Osuna immediately suspected a trick, but Mendoza kept on groaning. He blurted that he was in agony, had to vomit. Still wary, Osuna pulled off the road and on to a clear patch by the river. With a warning that he would shoot Mendoza if he tried to escape, Osuna unlocked the handcuffs.

The prisoner stumbled out, heaving. He took two or three steps before collapsing on his back. Osuna loosened the revolver in its holster - he wasn't going to be fooled. A minute passed, and Mendoza remained motionless. Osuna leaned over him.

Like lightning, Mendoza's hand snaked to his boot. A knife flashed. He stabbed once, twice, three times. Osuna reeled backwards, blood welling between the fingers he held to his chest. Mendoza seized the revolver. He kicked Osuna, rolling him to the river's edge. As he entered the water, close to death, Miguel Osuna's last thoughts were of his family.

Mercifully he did not feel the razor teeth of the seething piranhas that would soon reduce him to a skeleton.

Aboard *Sea Shepherd* the days slipped smoothly by, like the ocean. The youngsters had settled down to a regular routine: sleep, food, lessons, emergency drills, experiments in the ship's laboratories - and always some fun. Friendships deepened, but Darren remained the outsider.

Gary and Susan still talked about the time they had seen him leaving the radio room, and they hadn't forgotten the ticking off from Leslie Curtis. But neither of them mentioned the incident to anybody else. Since then Curtis had gone out of his way to be pleasant. He even apologised for speaking sharply, explaining that he had been busy and harassed. Darren too seemed to be making an effort. It was quite a surprise when he greeted Gary with a mumbled 'Hello' on deck.

Although puzzled by the radio room affair, Gary thought little of it. Not so Susan. She wasn't one to bear a grudge, and had accepted Curtis's apology; but however hard she tried, she just could not bring herself to like the man. She didn't trust him either. His switched-on smile and strained good humour made her wince.

Now the students were crowding eagerly into *Sea Shepherd*'s main laboratory. They goggled...weird and multicoloured specimens in tanks, underwater viewing windows, microscopes, purring machines, boffins wearing long white coats.

Ben beckoned Yves and Vanessa, who appeared more interested in each other than in what he was saying. 'Take a look at this.' He lifted the lid of a huge tank. All the youngsters pressed forward. 'We caught that yesterday,' Bellingham added. 'Anyone tell me what it is?'

Norman's answer was blotted out by a loud exclamation from the naturalist. 'Don't touch!' He grabbed Yves' wrist. 'If that thing stings you, you'll be hopping up and down for a week. More than one swimmer has been stung to death by a Portuguese man-of-war.'

They all stared at the foot-long, bright-blue body with its yards of tentacles. 'The blue bit is a gas-filled float,' Bellingham told them, 'and the long poisonous tentacles are for fishing. There are two shorter sets of tentacles - one used to digest food, the other in reproduction. Actually it's not a single creature but hundreds working together.'

Then, unexpectedly, the normally silent Darren asked: 'Why's it called a Portuguese man-of-war?'

'Good question,' Ben replied. 'See the sail on top of the float? It reminded old-time mariners of the Portuguese man-of-war sailing ship.'

Norman spoke up again, contributing the information that a gaudy little fish named Nomeus lives among the tentacles, immune to their sting, and shares its host's food. Ben confirmed this. 'But if the fish is wounded, it too gets eaten. By the way, there's just one other animal which dares to tangle with the Portuguese man-of-war -

that's the loggerhead turtle. I've seen a turtle, its eyes swollen shut from stings, munching away at its attacker as if it were a salad.'

Next their attention turned to a row of large jars. The faces leering back at them through the glass resembled something out of science fiction. Susan felt her flesh creep, and moved closer to Gary. Pickled in alcohol were the grisly remains of carnivorous creatures from the 'abyss' - the darkest deepest realms of the sea. Creatures that were never meant to see the day. Some were snake-like, others round as plates, most had long needle-sharp teeth and mouths that were enormous compared with their bodies.

In the eternal night of the abyss, certain inhabitants are blind. But many are equipped with bulging eyes or wear luminous spots. This light attracts their food and their mates. Sometimes sailors find strange corpses floating on the waves - fish swept up from the deep, possibly by an underwater eruption. Often they burst as they rise to the surface. The gases in their bodies expand when the pressure is reduced. 'Down there, the pressure is thousands of times greater than on the surface.' Ben's audience was spellbound.

'The underwater world has hardly been charted - less so than the moon. We know startlingly little about the 310 million cubic miles of ocean covering seven-tenths of the globe.'

He went on to describe some of the marvels man *had* discovered: mountains to match Everest, valleys that would swallow the Grand Canyon six times over, plains carpeted in 12,000 feet of mud.

'The sea's average depth is $2^1/_2$ miles, but in places it is seven miles. These trenches, unchanged for millions of years, each contain unique life forms. And that's where governments want to dump toxic chemicals and radioactive waste!'

Bellingham looked heavenwards.

After responding to their comments, he ushered the youngsters out.

A few minutes later Ben joined Captain James Alexander on *Sea Shepherd*'s bridge to discuss the next day's schedule. They were soon so engrossed that they didn't spot Curtis hovering in the background.

When Alexander caught sight of the radio officer he broke off in mid-sentence...'Yes, Leslie?'

'Message for you, Captain.'

Alexander scanned the paper he was handed. 'Dammit! What are they playing at?'

Bellingham cocked an inquiring eyebrow.

The captain took his arm. 'Better come with me, Ben. This affects you too.'

In the radio room, Bellingham struggled to keep a straight face. Mild-mannered Alexander could be very outspoken at times - as someone at the other end of the radio already knew. That someone was Sir Charles Fotheringay, chairman of the Conservation Committee in London.

Alexander's tone conveyed a mixture of irritation and disbelief: 'Let's get this straight, Sir Charles. You want to fly out a security specialist...not even a navy man...to protect us on the voyage. From what? Think we're going to be mugged by a sea monster? *I'm* master of this ship, responsible for safety. I don't need help - particularly from intruders.'

Sir Charles sighed. The sound was quite audible over the radio. He respected Alexander, a first-rate captain. If only he weren't so stubborn. 'Look, Jim. The committee has heard rumours, nothing definite, that certain commercial groups are set on thwarting The Eden Mission. And they may not be too fussy about how they do it...'

Alexander: 'Sabotage, you mean?'

Fotheringay: 'It's possible. So we mustn't take any chances, must we? Hence the security man. He's ex-SAS, a top operator. I can personally vouch for him. Incidentally, I gather you've got young Vanessa Pilgrim on board. Her father is Leonard Pilgrim, the financier, a prominent member of the committee who has been extremely generous to the conservation cause.'

Alexander glanced quickly at Bellingham.

Fotheringay added: 'I hope you'll co-operate, Jim. Otherwise the students and teachers will have to come home...'

Up on deck, Susan pointed in delight. 'Oh...how lovely! Dolphins!' Gary, Norman, Vanessa and Yves followed her as she ran. Riding the ship's bow wave were a dozen or more of them - black with white chins, chests and bellies, bands of grey and yellow on the flanks. Water sprayed from their long beaks and dorsal fins as these enchanting acrobats arced through the air.

'*Delphinus delphis,*' Norman observed, 'the common dolphin. One of the whale family.'

Susan hung over the ship's rail. 'They're jumping for joy.' Her blue eyes danced.

'Not really,' corrected Norman. 'It's a way of saving energy.'

For a moment Susan contemplated pushing him overboard. Know-all!

Gary put his arm round her waist. 'Super, aren't they? Shame so many have to die. Drowned in tuna nets, hunted for food, killed to stop them eating fish.'

Vanessa chipped in: 'We studied dolphins at school. They're supposed to be very kind to each other - especially if one's in distress - and they've been known to save swimmers from drowning... What do you think, Yves?'

Yves went on watching the acrobatics display. 'Wish I knew more about them. All I remember is dolphins can sleep with one eye open, and they get stomach ulcers if they worry.'

Susan, speaking up for Norman's benefit, announced: 'A dolphin's brain weighs 1,700 grammes, 250 more than a human's. Some scientists claim dolphins are at least as intelligent and ethical as we are.'

She waited, hoping Norman would react. He did: 'I doubt it.'

Instantly Susan retorted: 'Well, Norman, obviously no animal could be as brainy as *you*...'

Meanwhile, in the radio room, Alexander and Bellingham concluded a hasty conference. Ben considered it wise to have a security specialist aboard. Alexander grudgingly agreed that it couldn't do any harm, and contacted London. 'You win, Sir Charles.

But I expect *everyone* on *Sea Shepherd* to obey my orders. When does he arrive?'

The unseen Fotheringay grinned wolfishly. 'Thank you, Jim. Johnny Masterson was flown in to the Azores today. He'll be helicoptered out to you by late afternoon.'

A cabin was prepared for the new passenger, whose coming presence caused lively speculation throughout the ship.

On his way back from checking the helicopter landing pad, First Officer Philip Grant bumped into a startled Curtis and Darren as they emerged from behind a lifeboat. The pair had been lost in conversation.

Grant walked on. He thought about the radio officer, not an easy person to get to know. Still, Curtis seemed to have made a friend in that boy - and, by all accounts, Darren was a bit of a loner. So it was good the two hit it off. Grant rubbed his cheek, cold and wet. A gusty wind was snatching handfuls of white from the wave-tops and herding clouds across the sombre sky. Rough weather ahead?

In the next hour the sea grew surlier. The ship began to pitch and roll. Susan, never the best of sailors, retired to her bunk. Vanessa visited the cabin. She was sympathetic, covering Susan with an extra blanket and giving her an anti-seasickness pill. When she was sure Susan was as comfortable as possible, Vanessa left. First, though, she put on an anorak.

Susan missed the excitement of Johnny Masterson's arrival. But the others gathered to see the helicopter clattering out of the gloom. For several minutes it hung in the air, like an indecisive insect. Too risky to land, the pilot must have judged.

The spectators craned their necks, then cheered as Masterson appeared, a kit bag over his shoulder, and was winched down on to the deck.

Vanessa eyed the newcomer approvingly: tall, dark, rugged. Noting her expression, Yves regarded Masterson with less enthusiasm. But he had to admit there was something instantly likeable about the man, something strong and reassuring.

The helicopter departed.

Captain Alexander shook Johnny's hand, and First Officer Grant showed him to his quarters.

Ben Bellingham was absent from the welcoming party, busy with grimmer matters. Satellite bulletins from around the world indicated that The Eden Mission was running into trouble. Various conservation teams reported the loss of movie cameras, a near-fatal mishap to two divers when their breathing apparatus failed, unexplained fires on boats and in observation huts... Accidents? Some, maybe. But surely not all.

That evening, on the bridge, Bellingham voiced his misgivings to Alexander. The captain nodded gravely. Perhaps Masterson *would* prove useful.

As Alexander went off duty he noticed the bobbing flicker of ships' lights far to port and starboard.

Sea Shepherd ploughed on towards Miami.

4 All ashore

Susan opened her arms, as if to greet a long-lost friend. The sun had returned - not the half-hearted, hide-and-seek sun of recent weeks. No, this was the real thing, pure gold pouring out of a perfect sky. She felt the warmth seeping deep into her skin.

Slowly the shore floated forward to meet them, or so it seemed. Miami! Without asking, she helped herself to the binoculars hanging round Gary's neck. Fumbling, she adjusted the focus. She wanted to see *everything*.

Susan gave a little grunt of pleasure: white sand, palm trees, high hotels whose reflecting windows signalled like lighthouses, elegant yachts leaning on the wind and combing creamily through the smooth blue water.

Blue! The sea was so blue! Travel brochure-blue. Susan gazed in wonder. Could this be the same Atlantic whose grey-green waves had made her stomach churn and driven her into her bunk?

She handed back Gary's binoculars. Both were shading their eyes. The sun shone everywhere, from above and from below, sparking silver on the water, teeming and gleaming like a shoal of surfacing fish...

'Warm enough for you?' Ben Bellingham stood between them. 'Temperature's in the nineties on the mainland.'

They chatted for a minute or two. 'Look, there's a pelican.' Ben pointed. 'A brown pelican, quite common around the Florida coast. People love watching their antics.'

41

The big bird, which reminded Gary of a pterodactyl, was making a reconnaissance flight parallel to *Sea Shepherd*. Suddenly the pelican plunged. A splash, a quick gobbling movement, and another fat fish was stored away in the bird's expandable throat pouch.

'Pelicans use their elastic bills as scoop-nets,' Ben explained. 'And they vary the height of their dive depending on the depth of the fish. Eat two pounds a day, those fellas, a quarter of their body weight.'

The bird came in to land on an old jetty. Now it looked clumsy, swaying and teetering down invisible steps to alight on flat webbed feet. Soon after, a dishevelled chick was rummaging in the adult's beak.

'Must have a nest nearby,' commented Bellingham. He shook himself. 'Well, gotta be going. I'll see you again before we disembark. By the way, better alter your watches - it's 9.10 local time, five hours behind England.'

The bear-like naturalist shambled away. To think Susan had once felt shy, almost frightened of meeting him!

She sensed, rather than saw, a new presence and peeked sideways. It was Yves. He was draped over the ship's rail and looked about as happy as someone being seasick. Why so glum?

Susan's eyes took in the scene farther along the deck. Ah, that was it. Vanessa. Wearing a polka-dot sun-suit that showed off her slender figure and shapely legs. Talking to Johnny Masterson, the handsome he-man security officer, in khaki shirt and shorts. Obviously enjoying themselves. Poor Yves!

The pelican had resumed its patrol. Susan inched nearer to Yves. 'Hello,' she said lightly. 'See the pelican? Betcha it catches something in a minute.' Yves lifted his head. Immediately the pelican obliged with a spectacular swoop. 'Told you, didn't I?' Susan chirped.

Yves feigned interest, but his face let him down. Susan switched her gaze from the bird to Yves, from Yves to Vanessa, and back to Yves. The pelican flapped off. 'Never mind,' she murmured, 'there are plenty more fish in the sea.'

By now a pilot had come aboard and was guiding the ship into Biscayne Bay, Miami's huge harbour where the water traffic never stops.

Gary found ports irresistible: the sights, the sounds, the smells. Sniffing the salty sunshiny air, he revelled in a constantly changing panorama. Ships everywhere - arriving, departing, resting - flying a rainbow range of flags. Vessels from the seven seas. Tugs busybodied back and forth, clearing their throats self-importantly. Lines of luxury cruisers, tethered side by side, nuzzled and nudged in the soft swell. Contentedly Gary listened to the chorus of ships' horns...mooing, bleating, catcalling.

A speedboat tore across the harbour in a flurry of foam. Another craft, slightly larger, charged after it. Gary watched.

On *Sea Shepherd*'s bridge the pilot ceased chewing to observe: 'Drug boat. Being chased by Customs.'

Captain Alexander spilt his coffee.

'Yeah,' continued the pilot. 'Welcome to Miami! Cocaine capital of the USA.' He scowled. 'Drug smuggling is Florida's number one industry, worth billions of dollars a year. I used to like living here. Not any more...'

Alexander was all ears.

The pilot grumbled on, warming to his subject. Corrupt politicians and police as well as drug barons were growing rich from the illegal trade. Cocaine, processed in secret Amazon jungle laboratories, was flown or shipped out of Peru, Colombia and Bolivia. Often it reached Miami via the neighbouring Bahamas. A highly organized network, including 'respectable' businessmen in both North and South America, ensures that the flow of cocaine never dries up.

'You can't trust anyone these days,' the pilot concluded, 'the world's gone money-mad.'

What happened next brought a gasp from Alexander. A tug towing a tanker had shed its line, and the bulky vessel was veering round out of control. The pilot cursed. 'She'll hit us for sure!'

Alexander's brain raced. He barked orders. Engines pounded.

The drifting ship loomed. There was some swift and skilful manoeuvring as *Sea Shepherd* took evasive action. In time? No... Yes...Just! Disaster averted by seconds.

The pilot thumped Alexander on the back. 'Damn tanker coulda wrecked us. That tug-boat skipper better be a good talker.'

Around Biscayne Bay many had witnessed the near collision. But none paid more attention than the man in the cockpit of a red seaplane. Now his curled lip registered contempt, frustration. He spoke rapidly into a radio. The aircraft taxied for take off; built up speed; then, as if the water were glue, finally wrenched itself free to gain altitude. Next stop: Houston, Texas.

Sea Shepherd started to sidle up to the quay. In the lecture hall, Bellingham addressed the assembled party.

'Our young conservationists will be assigned to project groups. We have a great deal to do and time is tight, so I'll need complete co-operation from *all* of you.'

The ship would serve as a moored hotel. But when field-work took teams too far from Miami, they would stay in alternative accommodation.

Ben Bellingham made his last remarks to the youngsters, telling them it was vital to stick with their team-leaders. 'Not least because there are some people about who oppose The Eden Mission...'

Three million acres of squelchy marshland, under which an inches-deep river oozes to the sea. It doesn't sound very appealing. It doesn't look very appealing on the map. Yet, as Susan was soon to discover first hand, the Florida Everglades is a kind of paradise.

Sitting in a hut with the others - Norman, Darren, Maude Mimpriss and Johnny Masterson - Susan wriggled her toes impatiently. The wildlife warden's lecture was interesting enough, but she could hardly wait to get out and explore for herself.

Susan only half heard the warden's words, her imagination already running free... Alligators basking on banks or staying submerged away from the midday sun, or bellowing in the mating season to attract females and warn off rival males. Aristocratic bald eagles whose nests could be 9½ feet across, twenty feet deep and weigh more than three tons. Ospreys crashing down from the blue to hook fish on their talons. Venomous water snakes. Finicky racoons, with black rings under their eyes as though they'd had too many late nights, washing their food thoroughly before eating it. Rare Florida pumas, fewer than thirty left. And, of course, the threatened manatees which naturalists are fighting to safeguard...

'Any questions?' The warden's gravelly voice. Susan blinked, hoping he hadn't noticed her daydreaming.

Relieved, she heard Norman ask: 'Are there lots of conservation problems?'

The warden stuck his thumbs in his belt. 'Yup. Plenty.'

He drew their attention to the map on the wall behind him. 'The shaded area at the bottom is a National Park, a wildlife sanctuary. But the rest of the Everglades, the bigger part, is unguarded.' Men have wrought havoc there - draining the land for farming, industry, holiday homes and leaving a legacy of pesticides and pollution. Fires sometimes rage on the parched earth. And more and more animals are being killed in traffic accidents. 'Alligator Alley, a 75-mile road that traverses the Everglades north of Miami, is a potential death-trap to any creature unwise enough to cross it.'

Then he added: 'Even here, drug smugglers operate. Guys landing in private planes, full of the stuff, where they can't be seen.'

He hitched up his trousers. 'We're gonna change all that, clean the place up.'

The warden outlined a multi-million-dollar, government-sponsored plan to restore the Everglades to their former wild wet splendour. The plan includes re-flooding thousands of acres and building a special highway - with underpasses just for the pumas!

'People will be paid well when they have to move. Some of 'em hate the idea. They'll try to make it tough for us. But, heck, we'll win.'

Miss Mimpriss put on her sun-hat - which made her look like an overgrown baby, Susan thought. Mimpriss led the visitors outside.

Their two-day tour of the Everglades was beginning.

Later the memories would be mounted like snapshots in Susan's mind. But now events moved as fast as an adventure film.

First there was the trip on an airboat, beyond the Park boundaries. A *real* Red Indian, a Miccosukee from the local reservation, helped them aboard the flat-bottomed craft. Although he wore a check shirt, jeans and sneakers, Susan had a fleeting vision of him proudly riding a bare-backed pony across a great plain browsed by huge herds of buffalo. What days those must have been...!

A piercing shriek brought back the present. Maude Mimpriss had somehow managed to lose her footing and get her feet wet. Susan was racked by giggles, which set Norman off. Even dour Darren sniggered. The youngsters took their places at the front of the boat. Johnny Masterson sat behind them, trying to console a damp and displeased teacher.

The Indian, perched high in the stern, started the aero-engine whose powerful propeller blast would blow them like the wind over the shallow water.

With a roar and a whoosh they were under way!

Hair streaming, Susan stared ahead. The marshy landscape rushed towards her, then passed in a dizzying blur. Reeds fell back as if scared by the boat's bullying approach. She was tempted to reach out and touch them, but she knew they could cut her hands badly.

On impulse, Susan swivelled round - and saw Miss Mimpriss squirm. A little green lizard, flung up from the water, was scrabbling for a hold on her bare arm. The startled teacher let go of her sun-hat. It flew away like a paper bag in a gale. She was not having a good day!

The boat slowed and with it the sliding scenery: trees, islands, stretches of dry ground.

A deer showed its face for a second, then its tail, then vanished. The Indian cut the engine. Nearby, alighting ducks skidded across the shiny surface like water-skiers. And great white herons stalked the shallows, gulping and guzzling molluscs.

Turning carefully, Susan surveyed this strangely enchanted wilderness through binoculars. A roseate spoonbill! Wow! Tall and stately, white head, body beautifully tinted pink and red, waggling its broad grey bill in the mud and water until touch told it to snap shut on shrimps or fish. How could people have hunted such birds, just to make fans from their wings?

A sudden growl - the boat's engine leapt to life. Off again. Though she couldn't see them, Susan imagined the cold coils of water snakes winding and unwinding in a remote mangrove swamp...

Someone, something touched her. She flinched, as if she'd been bitten. 'Norman!' He grinned behind those familiar glasses. Meant no harm. Just being friendly, sharing his pleasure in today's excursion.

Up ahead Susan spotted a falcon. Yes...a peregrine falcon, beginning its deadly dive, unerring as a guillotine. She pitied the doomed prey. Gary was nuts about peregrines. Why wasn't he here now, instead of with another team? She missed him. Still, they'd be together before long.

The Indian switched off the noisy engine, letting the boat drift along a channel of deeper water. He pointed. Two alligators, one making a meal of a green turtle. Susan looked away. Norman reached for his camera.

Of all those on board, only Susan noticed they were not alone. A second airboat had silently appeared. Standing in the bow was a man with a video camera. He seemed to be filming *them*, not the wildlife. Odd. For some reason, Susan felt uneasy...

Abruptly the other airboat powered off, disturbing the alligators. The *Sea Shepherd* party headed back to base - and a late lunch - soon after.

Now for the next Everglades experience: puma tracking. Susan knew Norman could hardly wait, and she assumed Darren was equally keen. But, of course, he hadn't said so. If only Darren would speak...Susan sensed that he wanted to, but *something* was stopping him.

Maude Mimpriss displayed no enthusiasm for pumas. She didn't care that they were endangered. What about her? She was clearly nervous of coming within a mile of the carnivorous cats - which measure five feet if you don't add on their thick, twitching tails. Then Johnny Masterson promised to protect her, and she bravely agreed to accompany the group.

She needn't have worried. Nobody saw so much as a whisker of the cats. Not even the naturalists who were keeping an eye, or rather an ear, on them through radio receivers. Bouncing along in a Jeep, Susan and the others heard how the pumas were tranquillised with drugged darts before being fitted with radio collars. Afterwards they could be tracked on the ground and from the air. Susan longed to catch just a *glimpse*...

That evening, she yawned her way through supper in *Sea Shepherd*'s dining-room. What a day! Sleepily Susan said goodnight and shuffled to the cabin. She'd have it to herself until Vanessa and company returned. Vanessa was quite nice - very nice, really. Funny how people grow on you. Susan gave her teeth the briefest of brushings, slipped into her night things and flopped down on the bunk. Soon be seeing Gary.

In her jumbled dreams, the man with the video camera stuck out his tongue. Suddenly it became a snake. The picture haunted her when she woke. But a bright new morning - plus a packed programme - banished gloomy thoughts.

Within two hours Susan was enjoying the view from an observation platform above the Everglades National Park. Open-mouthed she watched an osprey in action. Claws dug deep into his captured prize, the dripping fish-hawk struggled skywards. Not far off, his mate and ravenous chicks waited restlessly in a leaf-lined nest the size of a double bed.

The warden beside Susan chuckled. 'Worth coming, uh?' She nodded. 'See how he holds the fish's head forwards,' said the warden. 'To reduce air resistance.'

Then, out of nowhere, an enormous white-helmeted bald eagle burst on to the scene.

'Hey, that's not fair!' Susan exclaimed. 'He's pinched the

osprey's fish!

Norman protested too. The warden shrugged. 'Sorry to say America's national bird - our emblem - is a lazy, bad-tempered bandit.'

But soon Susan was cheering. Undeterred, the osprey had plummeted again - splashed, struck, and ferried the catch safely home. His mate tore it into strips and fed the young.

Norman and Susan asked the warden for more information. 'Sure!' Ospreys occasionally drown when they sink their talons into big fish and are pulled under...they build their nests high to try to foil egg-thieving rats and racoons...and they were once almost wiped out by pesticides.

'DDT was the culprit, sprayed on marshes to control mosquitoes. It led to the ospreys laying thin-shelled eggs which wouldn't hatch. The pesticide doesn't dissolve in water but concentrates in fatty tissues. Microscopic organisms absorb it, then plants, then the fish that eat *them* and so on. At each stage of the food chain, the effect multiplies dramatically. The DDT dose in ospreys was 100 million times greater than in the water...'

Reluctantly the youngsters left, boarded a boat and set out to search for manatees. Would the shy aquatic mammals show themselves? The guide promised nothing. But in the late afternoon, a bristly grey head popped up amid some weeds. Susan nearly fell overboard. It was so...*ugly!*

Never win a beauty contest - that's for sure, Gary decided. He was peering down from an anchored launch 250 miles away. The manatee, which had surfaced for air, promptly submerged into the clear green waters of Crystal River. Gary felt slightly embarrassed, as though the unlovely beast could read his thoughts. Besides, looks aren't everything - and Gary had grown quite fond of manatees in the last couple of days while working with Ben Bellingham's group.

Has Susan seen one yet? he wondered. If not, how would he describe it to her?   An overstuffed, ten-foot-long sausage with

49

flippers and a flat tail. Beady-eyed, snub-nosed, hare-lipped, moustached, no external ears, no front teeth, forever feeding its funny face. A 2,000-pound specimen will tuck away as much as 200 pounds of water plants each day. Elephant-coloured, it belonged to jumbo's tribe, so scientists said.

Were *these* the animals that sailors, including Christopher Columbus, had called mermaids? Must've needed their eyes tested. Gary could find no resemblance whatever between a manatee - helpless on land - and a seductive creature, half woman, half fish, sitting on a rock combing her hair and suckling a child. Other mariners had referred to manatees as sirens - sweet-singing temptresses who lured ships to destruction. Again, hard to imagine, since manatees can only squeak and croak. But even now, they are officially classified as 'Sirenians'. Maybe mermaid legends came about because the female of the species sometimes sits up in the water with a nursing calf supported by her flipper...

Gary stretched. He'd got a lot to tell Susan. Yesterday morning Gary and the team had helped save a 'mermaid' from dying. At least, he hoped so. With the Florida Marine Patrol, they had gone to the aid of an injured mother manatee off the coast. Blood was gushing from deep gashes in her back, caused by a speedboat propeller. If she died, the baby swimming beside her would perish too.

Four men succeeded in netting her; the calf was caught by hand. A crane hoisted the haemorrhaging manatee on to a stretcher. While a biologist gave her antibiotics injections, Yves and Vanessa bathed the wounds. Gary noted approvingly that Vanessa wasn't squeamish, and he was glad that she and Yves were good friends again. Before long, mother and baby had been lifted into a truck - bound for an oceanarium. There, with luck, they would both survive and thrive.

'I've seen worse,' said the biologist. 'A head blow...fatal. And a ship's propeller could have cut her almost in half.'

Throughout that day the marine patrol performed more rescues. Two young bullies in a boat were found tormenting a manatee calf with metal poles. As soon as they sighted the patrol, the youths

50

jettisoned the evidence of their cruelty and tried to act innocent. But they'd been photographed. No escaping a stiff fine. 'Serves 'em right!' Gary had muttered as their boat was towed to shore.

Later, in a quiet estuary, the patrol surprised a poacher intent on killing his cornered victim. The man got away, but so did the manatee.

Gary, Vanessa and Yves were learning a good deal about manatees, also known as sea cows. They have suffered severely at human hands. Hunted for meat, oil and hides, they make easy targets. Only three species - the Caribbean, the West African and the South American River Manatee - still exist; as well as the closely related dugong, which inhabits the Indo-Pacific region. All are in decline. One of their kin, a 24-ton giant named Steller's Sea Cow, was discovered in 1742 when Russian navigator Captain Vitus Bering was exploring what is now the Bering Sea. Just 27 years later, the whole population had been slaughtered - Steller's Sea Cow gone for ever.

'Florida has a thousand or so manatees. We intend to look after them...'

The biologist's words came back to Gary next day, aboard the anchored launch in Crystal River. Everybody here sought to save manatees, but it was no easy task. These vulnerable creatures face a variety of hazards. Pollution, dredging and waterside building developments rob them of their food supply; drainage schemes destroy their habitat; canal locks can trap them. They may also die from drowning or starvation when flippers become entangled in crab-pot lines.

Gary picked his way across the launch's deck and went below. Through the boat's glass bottom he kept watch on four manatees snoozing by a warm-water spring that bubbled from the river bed. A big male rolled over for a scratch. A calf woke its mother to play and hitch a ride upwards for another breath. Mermaids or not, they weren't short of charm.

Gary returned to the deck. Ben Bellingham stood alone several yards away. He had been unusually subdued lately, worried and

withdrawn. What was bothering him? Gary guessed, correctly...
The Eden Mission and its enemies.

5 Sharks

Gloria Benton closed the sliding glass door and tip-tapped to the balcony's edge. Kicking off her high-heeled shoes, she inhaled deeply and gazed out over the prosperous city of Houston. Phew! She needed a break from the angry men in the smoke-filled apartment behind her. Art, her husband, had lost his temper. And so had more than one of his business associates, gathered for a hastily called meeting. She didn't understand what was going on. But if it caused Art to shout, it must be serious...

Indoors, Maximilian Kruger pointed an accusing finger at Benton. '*You* told me we had nothing to fear from The Eden Mission, said it was no match for the organization. Why are these do-gooders still nosing around, stirring things up, spoiling trade? It's time they were squashed.'

A fat Brazilian cocaine-dealer named Gomez echoed the German's sentiments: 'Yeah. Stop pussyfooting, get rid of the snoopers for keeps.'

Benton's knuckles went white as he fought to take a grip of himself. 'We've gotta be careful,' he warned. 'Look, this is a global game, spreading as far south as Antarctica. The organization holds all the high cards. It's playing them one by one, and it's winning. Our people are everywhere - even in the ecologists' camp - watching, reporting, telling us where and when to strike next. There's no way we can lose.'

Be patient, he urged Gomez, reminding him of future assaults on

53

the conservation movement.

Gomez remained unconvinced. Sneering, he referred to the bungled collision attempt in Miami harbour.

Benton's control snapped. He banged the arm of his chair. 'OK, the crash failed. What do you suggest - blow up the ship?'

'Sounds good to me,' Gomez retorted.

Benton smiled mirthlessly. 'Great! Make heroes of the creeps... all those dead kids...bring the press and police swarming like flies. Just what the organization needs! The Eden Mission is attracting enough publicity already.'

He added in a calmer tone: 'And remember, not everyone on board is Bellingham's ally.'

Gomez dropped the argument, but Kruger took it up. Benton gritted his teeth.

When Kruger had finished, Benton replied quietly: 'Please listen to reason, Max. We've got the money, the power, the spies, the muscle. The conservationists don't know what's hitting 'em, and nobody can prove a thing against the organization. Let's keep it that way. If we have to get *really* rough, we will. Believe me.'

However, Kruger still wasn't satisfied, and a Japanese businessman made further objections.

Benton passed Kruger an ashtray. 'The Director has given specific instructions. Do you want to oppose his wishes?'

A hush descended on the meeting. Benton waited. 'Right, we'll vote. Those in favour of pursuing the present policy raise your hands.'

All but Kruger responded. Benton glanced at the German. 'I'm sure Max will abide by the majority decision,' he purred.

WELCOME TO SEA WORLD. Glimpsing the sign, Susan felt her heart skip. Pleasure...and a thrill and chill of anticipation. How often do you come face to face with bloodthirsty sharks - even if they're mouthing at the four-inch-thick glass that holds them back in a gigantic aquarium? Scary. A birthday treat to treasure. But what pleased Susan most was the prospect of seeing Gary again.

While the other youngsters criss-crossed Florida on conservation projects, she had been allowed to join her friend for a short visit to Sea World in Orlando. Gary and teachers Peter Stokes and Geoffrey Baggalley were already there, awaiting Susan and Johnny Masterson.

Johnny made some remark, which Susan rather rudely ignored. Her eyes searched the crowd at the pre-arranged meeting point. 'There he is!' She broke into a run. 'Gary!' 'Hello, Susan...Happy birthday!' To her surprise she was tongue-tied. Both had so much to say, so much news to share, but the words wouldn't come. He's brown, she thought, a tan suits him. Gary was thinking the same of her - the sun had given her skin a honey hue. I've never noticed how pretty she is.

'This is daft!' Susan declared. 'Behaving like strangers.' She threw her arms round Gary's neck and he hugged her. After that they couldn't stop talking.

Side by side, the three adults following, Gary and Susan set out for the aquarium and a promised 'Shark Encounter'. An accurate description, as Gary knew, but he wasn't going to tell Susan anything that might spoil the shock.

The friends fell silent. Did she share his vision of triangular fins cutting through the water towards them? Sharks - the perfect predators, lethal lords of the ocean for 400 million years. Fast, streamlined, relentless as homing torpedoes. Some species so aggressive they attack one another in the womb. Born ready for action, each equipped with 24 teeth to tear flesh. Later their fully-grown jaws can exert a pressure of twenty tons per square inch.

Sharks. They fascinated Gary. As a seven-year-old he had seen photographs of them, and ever since had shown a shark-like appetite for any book or film that would tell him more about the big 'bad' fish. But not all of the 370 species are big or bad. The smallest measures under three inches, and the largest - the sixty-foot whale shark - is harmless. Though most are cannibals. And a dozen, notably the gruesome great white, are man-eaters...

A tug at his sleeve. Susan - radiating excitement. SHARK ENCOUNTER was straight ahead. With Messrs. Masterson, Baggalley and Stokes close behind, the teenagers went in.

Susan 'goose-pimpled'. Any moment now! Then, to her disappointment, she discovered she must delay saying a breathless hello to the sharks. First there was an information film to sit through. However, the disappointment didn't last. The pictures and commentary were to cast a spell over Susan - and would nearly put her off swimming in the sea for life...

Enter the arch-villain, expressionless eyes, two-inch teeth exposed in a cruel crescent sneer, undisputed champion of terror. The great white. No other creature can rival it for sheer ferocity. Nothing but death will halt its headlong charge. A thirty-foot great white strikes with the full force of its 8,000 pounds, ripping chunks from its victims or biting clean through. Its hunger - or greed - seems insatiable. A horse has been found in a great white's belly. Another's contained two seven-foot sharks, and a third the remains of a thirsty elephant which ran into Kenyan coastal waters.

Susan squeezed Gary's hand. Not simply out of affection, he knew, smiling to himself in the dark.

The film rolled on. For some great whites, apparently, human flesh is top of the menu - an acquired taste they keep trying to satisfy.

Sharks are at their most ravenous when the water temperature reaches 70 degrees Fahrenheit. It's then that they may go on the rampage in a 'feeding frenzy', triggered perhaps by bait or entrails dumped overboard from a fishing boat. At such times the sharks' blood-lust knows no bounds as they snap and slash at anything - each other, even a whirling propeller. Any person caught up in this dance of death can only pray for a swift end.

Gary recalled stories he had read of shark attacks, stories he would never tell his soft-hearted friend. Like the night the *Nova Scotia*, a troop-ship, was sunk off South Africa in 1942. A thousand men perished, and dawn revealed the legless bodies of many of them floating on the surface. And in 1930, spectators at a yacht race in Port Phillip Bay, Australia, watched helplessly as a shark savaged nineteen-year-old Norman Clark. Clark had dived off a pier. He was immediately seized by the shark, which hurled him into the air, bit off his legs and played with him like a cat with a mouse. Finally, tiring of its game, the shark grabbed Clark round the waist and disappeared with him...

The on-screen drama was as gripping as any thriller. Beside Gary, Susan sat enthralled. A tiger shark produces and sheds 24,000 teeth in ten years, a blue shark can travel at over forty miles an hour, a mako shark will sometimes chase boats and jump on board. Then came the information that sharks will swallow seals, turtles, birds, lobsters, rubbish and coal. Biologists, dissecting one bloated brute, pulled out three overcoats, a car number-plate and a chicken coop...

Although Susan's enthusiasm would never equal Gary's, she now understood why he was hooked on the fearsome fish. Almost indestructible, even after being disembowelled they are still dangerous, still programmed to attack and kill. A particularly voracious man-eater has established itself in Central America's Lake Nicaragua, migrating from the Caribbean.

They are found everywhere. In warm or cold seas, deep or shallow waters, rivers... Men, women and children have all fallen victim to those terrible teeth.

Sharks have few enemies: other sharks, swordfish, killer whales - and, of course, man who hunts them for food and sport.

'Just a few more minutes,' Gary whispered in Susan's ear. 'Then you'll see the real thing.'

Suddenly her concentration began to waver. She'd taken in so much - surprising, shocking, sensational. Now her thoughts focused on the waiting aquarium.

Conveniently the screen turned black. The lights rose. Susan stood and breathed out a soundless whistle. Then, dragging Gary with her and unceremoniously treading on toes, she hurried from the cinema. Masterson, Stokes and Baggalley could barely keep up.

Shark Encounter would be everything Susan imagined - and more. Standing on a 'people-mover', like a conveyor belt, they travelled slowly along a glass tunnel at the bottom of the aquarium. Surrounded by sharks. Beside you, above you, behind, ahead. You're in their domain. Lemon sharks, sand tigers, bull sharks, brown sharks, nurse sharks - some fierce, some placid - cruising and banking with effortless magnificence through three million litres of man-made salt water. Well fed, they don't turn on each other. 'They're...beautiful!' Susan exclaimed. Gary obviously agreed. He reminded her that *Jaws 3* was filmed here. This caused her to think again of the shark as merciless aggressor. But she still marvelled at its beauty...

Eventually, dazed and dazzled, Susan emerged into Sea World's sunshine. Crowds of tourists swarmed as thickly as ever. She walked ahead of Gary and the adults, her mind swimming with the sharks. Gary quickened his pace. He drew near...then choked. A shout stuck in his throat.

Somebody - a swarthy man - had jumped out at Susan and was bundling her off!

Johnny Masterson swore, rushed forward. The kidnapper and the girl were lost in the throng. 'Out of my way!' Masterson bellowed. He dodged and weaved between the dawdling visitors, shoved some aside, spied Susan for a second, started to gain ground.

Then Masterson went sprawling. A foot had shot sideways and tripped him. Not caring whose, he was up immediately. *Save Susan.* No sign of her. Masterson barged on, Gary and the teachers bringing up the rear.

At this point Susan took a hand - her kidnapper's hand - and bit it hard. The man yelped as she wriggled free. He managed to recapture her, but not without difficulty.

Catching sight of them, Masterson put on a final spurt. He vaulted a low wall. They were right in front of him.

As Gary arrived on the scene he saw Masterson's arm lunge - a punch? a chop? - and the swarthy man tumbled backwards. He lay very still, unconscious. Gary stared at Masterson admiringly,

58

and embraced a sobbing Susan.

Curious onlookers began to gather. Masterson bent down and, none too gently, tried to revive the unmoving kidnapper. A uniformed patrolman appeared and wanted to know what had happened. Why was the guy on the ground? Masterson rose and turned to explain. Susan, her nerves now steady, filled in the story.

Left out of things, with only the sheepish-looking teachers for company, Gary glared at the circle of tourists. He vaguely registered a grey car in the background. It was rolling closer. A saloon, its passenger door open. Suspicion sparked in his mind.

The kidnapper had recovered, was on his feet! He dashed through the bystanders like a sprinter. Masterson and the patrolman spun round. The car engine revved. Susan's assailant scrambled into the seat beside the driver. With tyres squealing, the saloon accelerated away - and nobody could stop it.

Several hundred miles to the east, off the Bahamas, a fishing boat's bows breasted the tinsel strips of sunlight strewn like decoration on a calm and cheerful sea. An ideal day for diving. The two men in wet-suits preparing to take the plunge were ecologists, whose boat had been specially adapted for survey duty. With a casual wave to their team-mates the black-clad figures dropped over the side. One carried an underwater camera.

Kicking their flippers and trailing a string of bubbles from their oxygen tanks, the divers descended deeper into a blue-green realm of light and shade and flitting shadows. Around them vivid platoons of fish wheeled and scattered. Below, throbbing with luminous colour, stretched the coral reef. Soon they would find the answer to an important question.

On the silver-streaked surface the boat swayed lazily, but those aboard were far from idle. Like the exploring frogmen, they too had only one concern: the coral reef. In the wheel-house, three conservationists pored over maps and charts whose dark markings represented ruined reefs around the world. The thought of it made the experts fume. Coral collecting for the souvenir trade, mining for construction material, pollution, nuclear testing...all agents of death among these living masterpieces. Reefs support a third of fish species, guard the land from erosion - and are more breathtaking than any work of art. Leaving the wheel-house, the naturalists went to help colleagues who were busy in other parts of the boat. Every mind pictured what was happening eighty feet beneath the water...

The leading diver gestured to his partner. Yes, the reef had been raided by coral hunters - a discarded net bag was evidence of that. The second man closed in with his camera. Farther on, the swimming investigators found traces of chemical and sewage pollution. Then they came upon a desert-like tract where mining had torn up the reef, carving jagged gaps. A graveyard that was once a pulsing rainbow of life.

The divers felt despondent. One of them leaned against a rock. Instantly a squat head shot out from a crevice. A moray eel, ten feet of steely sinew with teeth and jaws that can crack clams and pin a diver in an unbreakable grip. The frogman was not slow to vacate the eel's territory.

As the rubber-suited men swam on, they became aware that they were being tracked by an interested spectator: a sleek barracuda, perhaps six feet long. Not the friendliest of fish. Always hungry, it is attracted by bright flashing objects. Barracudas may steal the catch from a fishing spear, or zero in on an unsuspecting swimmer wearing a wrist-watch or a bracelet. And legs dangling from a raft can prove irresistible. Even beach-side waders have been ambushed. A barracuda bites only once, unlike a shark, and inflicts a clean straight wound quite different from the shark's ragged tear.

However, the divers were not alarmed. They halted. Their escort halted too, fixing them with a glassy stare. They stared back - until the barracuda, bored or bewildered, withdrew. But not far. Fascinated, the men watched the predator herding fish to the surface, and before long a faint rain of silver scales began to fall. Pretty, but slightly sad.

60

By now the reef explorers had almost completed their survey. A couple more minutes' filming, then they could ascend to the boat. In unison they propelled themselves forward...and together saw a totally unexpected sight.

Festooned in weed and ravaged by time and salt water, the dim outline was unmistakable. A ship. An old sailing ship. A Spanish galleon? Perhaps one of thousands lost in the Caribbean between the 16th and 18th centuries when the conquistadores plundered the vast wealth of Central and Southern America and were themselves robbed by storms, reefs and buccaneers? If so, tons of treasure worth a fortune might still be on board.

The divers wanted to investigate further. But they were not the first to discover the wreck. Indeed, twenty or more frogmen were circling it in a ballet of bubbles. Beyond could be seen several indistinct shapes...containers, crates.

Intrigued, the cameraman let his film run. Was this a legal salvage operation? Or were these the modern-day pirates he'd heard of, some funded by the Mafia?

He was not left wondering long. Half a dozen figures detached themselves from the salvage group and advanced in formation, like a fighter squadron. The leader held a spear gun. Any doubts about his intentions were swiftly and violently dispelled. The spear pierced the cameraman's hand, the attacking force only yards away. Aiding his unconscious partner, the other diver tried to make an escape. Hopeless!

Then...a slow, rolling rumble. The seabed shook. Sand swirled, turning the water opaque. An earthquake beneath the waves.

Groggy but desperately determined, the diver struggled upwards, towing his friend and the camera. Would both reach the surface alive?

Good old *Sea Shepherd*! Susan led Gary, Stokes, Baggalley and Johnny Masterson up the ship's gangway. She'd had her fill of adventure; all she wanted now was a quiet life.

At the top of the gangway Radio Officer Leslie Curtis stepped smartly forward and saluted. Was he mocking her? Susan regarded him neutrally, unsure whether she would ever quite trust him. But his grin was broad and his handshake firm when he expressed relief at her safe return. 'Mr. Masterson phoned the captain with the news.' Susan summoned some insincere words in response. Curtis explained that her parents had been contacted and told the danger was past.

'He certainly seems pleased to see you,' murmured Gary as they moved on. Susan said nothing.

Moments later she was caught up in a scrum. The other youngsters, back from their field trips, mobbed her like a pop star. Susan the heroine! Intrepid survivor of the Orlando ordeal.

They demanded details. First, though, there were happy hellos. Vanessa kissed Susan's cheek, Yves ruffled her hair, Norman patted her on the back. But, oddly, it was the mumbled 'Glad you're all right' from Darren that meant most to her.

Meanwhile, in the captain's cabin, Alexander paced up and down while Ben Bellingham and First Officer Philip Grant sat conversing seriously. A rap at the door. 'Enter.' Alexander wasted no time on pleasantries as Masterson and the three teachers filed in. 'Please sit.' He glanced at his watch. 'Gentleman...and madam' - he nodded in the direction of Maude Mimpriss - 'you know why we're here. A nasty business. Could've been a lot nastier but for the prompt action of Mr. Masterson. Congratulations! Perhaps you'd bring us all up to date.'

Masterson stood and gave a brief summary of events at Sea World. 'I blame myself,' he concluded. 'If I'd been more alert...the kidnapper should never have got away. The police have his description and the car's, but I don't hold out much hope.'

Alexander spoke again: 'No need to reproach yourself, man. You did well. The thing is, what are *we* going to do now?'

Ben Bellingham's face was drawn. 'I'm worried,' he admitted. 'Very worried. I'll risk my neck for The Eden Mission any day, but I won't gamble on the safety of innocent young people. Who can tell what's in store? Our opponents are stepping up the pressure I had a report from Australia just an hour ago. Yes, I'm worried. Maybe the youngsters should go home.'

A heavy silence. Alexander ended it. 'Excuse me, Ben, there's nothing to connect this kidnapping with The Eden Mission. Why would anybody pick on her? The man who grabbed Susan, and his accomplice, may be nutcases.'

Bellingham took no part in the discussion which followed. Unlike Maude Mimpriss. In extremely agitated tones she aired her own anxieties.

Captain Alexander intervened. 'Let's not panic. I see no reason to send any of our passengers back to England. That would make us look stupid, weak - as though we can't cope. We *can* cope. By being extra vigilant. Mr. Masterson and I will work out a plan, a tight security system that everyone must stick to.' Alexander inclined his head towards Bellingham. 'What do you say, Ben?'

The naturalist's expression underwent a subtle change and the corners of his mouth twitched. 'You may be right, Jim. Anyway, I didn't fancy breaking the bad tidings to the youngsters - they'd probably have mutinied!'

On deck, Susan sprawled in a canvas chair next to Gary and closed her eyes. Too much, everything was a bit too much. Even the boisterous reunion had tired her out. Gary, she knew, understood this without needing to be told and she was grateful. Sleep began to wrap Susan like a cosy blanket.

Relaxing, Gary let his mind drift across Miami harbour - carried by the swelling sails of yachts or borne away on a luxury liner, stylish and spick and span, for a Caribbean cruise...

'Gary.' Susan's drowsy voice. So she hadn't dropped off. 'Gary.' More insistent.

'Uh-huh.' Regretfully he disembarked from his daydream and rejoined her. 'Well, go on then.'

Susan took her time. 'Er, remember what I said about the Everglades and the man in the airboat? You know, the one with the video camera?'

Gary quipped: 'Oh, yeah. He thought you were so gorgeous you ought to be in films.'

'Shut up, Gary, and listen. Suppose he *was* taking pictures of me, and suppose he passed them on to somebody else...?'

'Like who?'

'Like that thug at Sea World.'

There was no humour now in Gary's demeanour. 'Hmmm...I wonder. Not funny, is it?'

Susan laid her hand on his arm. 'Shall I tell Ben?'

Gary considered before replying: 'I dunno. Might be a false alarm. Besides, he's got plenty on his plate already. No, I don't think we should bother him.'

A resonant moan from *Sea Shepherd*'s funnel put an end to the conversation. They sauntered to the other side of the ship. On the quay, ropes were being cast off. The gangway had been hauled up. Gary recognised three crew members - boffins from the laboratories - who would be staying behind to play their part in the Save the Manatee project. Susan gave an unladylike holler and waved. The trio waved back.

Sea Shepherd was under way, beginning the next leg of her journey. Destination: San Pedro, California.

While Gary remained on deck, determined it seemed to count every ship and boat in Biscayne Bay, Susan went below for a nap. Two hours later, after a shower and a change of clothes, she made straight for the dining-room with Vanessa. Dinner. Susan's tummy rumbled; she'd never been hungrier.

She was about to sit beside Gary when Ben Bellingham claimed her. 'The captain and I would like the pleasure of your company,' he said, bowing. Wide-eyed she meekly accompanied him to the top of the table where he politely pulled out a chair and seated her by Captain Alexander, who soon insisted she call him Jim.

The meal had a festive atmosphere, and Susan was treated as guest of honour. Maude Mimpriss shed her inhibitions, for once.

A steward entered, bearing a silver bucket in which nestled a large green bottle. Gradually the hubbub subsided. Ben was on his feet. 'How about some champagne?' Another steward brought glasses. Alexander opened the bottle with a pop and a cascade of bubbly froth. The glasses were quickly filled, and Bellingham proposed a toast. 'Susan!' 'Susan!' they all repeated. Blushing, she tried her first taste of champagne. The bubbles tickled.

Gary watched her proudly before noting that there were fourteen chairs at the captain's table; the extra one was for Johnny Masterson. Silly to be superstitious, but Gary felt relieved - and optimistic about the coming days.

He slept soundly that night, waking in a sun-splashed cabin. A puddle of light lay on the floor by his bunk. Gary grunted. He *could* get up... Why rush?

'Hello there.' Two feet poking from pyjama trousers jerked into view, then the rest of Norman. 'We start lessons again today.'

'Terrific!' Gary burrowed under the sheets. 'I can't wait.'

By mid-morning he had decided school was OK. The teachers weren't bad either - considering they were teachers. But he was not sorry to put away his books.

When Gary took a pre-lunch stroll, Norman tagged along. Talk, talk, talk. The bespectacled boy made Gary's head ache. Would nothing stop him? As if in answer to a prayer, the words dried up. Norman gaped, pointing. An enormous silver-blue fish had rocketed out of the sea near the ship's bow. It 'swam' in the air for what seemed an age, burst back into the water and flung a glittering plume high over its shoulder.

A tuna. Plump but athletic on a diet of garfish, mackerel and squid - which gives it the unique taste so sought-after by humans. This one, if it evaded fishermen's nets and hooks, might build its weight to as much as a ton and its length to fourteen feet. Yet a tuna could outpace a flying fish.

Norman's tongue got back to work. 'Tunas, you know, never really stop moving. They can swim indefinitely. Biologists estimate that a fifteen-year-old specimen must have covered a million miles.'

Gary laughed - Norman was impossible. 'Thank you, Professor.'

In the data-processing centre, a large cabin next to the radio room,

65

green-printed messages flickered on screens: information about The Eden Mission's worldwide progress, or lack of it, sent by satellite. Ben Bellingham turned away from the screens and stared at First Officer Philip Grant. Both men were frowning. Grant shut the door behind them, and they set off along the corridor.

'Treasure hunters!' Bellingham almost spat. 'The two divers could've been killed. Thank God they escaped.'

Grant nodded. 'I can understand the salvors wanting to protect their haul. But murder...?'

They walked on, Bellingham trying to make sense of it. He couldn't. Maybe the divers' video would.

Sea Shepherd carved purposefully through the Caribbean, gobbling up the miles. Day soon faded into dusk and dusk into night. After dinner, Gary and Susan promenaded round and round the deck, reluctant to turn in. The sky was daisied with stars and moonlight meandered across the waves. How romantic! Perhaps it was this that inspired Susan to give Gary a more than affectionate kiss before parting.

In the cabin, she found her room-mate emptying drawers amid a litter of clothes. Vanessa, normally poised in all situations, looked flustered.

'What is it?' Susan asked, concerned.

'My watch - have you seen it?'

Susan visualised the delicate gold wrist-watch. 'No.' Her cheeks burned, as though she were being accused.

Vanessa took in Susan's discomfort. 'Oh, I didn't mean...you didn't think...' The older girl sighed. 'I don't know where it could have got to.'

Susan smiled. 'I'll help you.'

On their knees they sorted out the piles of belongings. The watch, Vanessa confided, was a present from her mother, who had died in a car crash.

Their search proved fruitless. Susan held Vanessa's hand. 'Never mind, it'll turn up.' Vanessa put on a brave face. 'You think so? Yves lost his pen - and that's still missing.'

Both girls remained kneeling. The idea of a thief on board was too unpleasant to contemplate. 'Let's tidy the cabin,' Susan suggested brightly.

It wasn't long before their quarters were shipshape again and Vanessa's composure returned. They sat down on the bottom bunk. 'Thanks,' said Vanessa. 'You know, you're nice-looking. Why don't you make more of yourself? A new hair-style, pretty dress, touch of make-up - you'd be quite a knock-out with all the boys.'

Susan shrugged.

Vanessa regarded this as a challenge. 'It's true. I'll show you.' For the next hour she had Susan changing clothes like a model. Vanessa's outfits were too big for the younger girl. But some of them, Susan saw in the full-length wardrobe mirror, did make her look...attractive. When Vanessa got busy with a comb and make-up, Susan didn't recognise herself. She giggled. Maybe she *should* take greater care over her appearance, but it was such a lot of bother.

Talk turned to boys. Was Gary Susan's boyfriend? Vanessa insisted on knowing. Susan gave a confused reply. No...yes...sort of. He was certainly her best friend. 'How about you and Yves?' Vanessa yawned. 'We'll see.'

The conversation continued in their bunks, and next morning they were both reluctant risers.

However, they weren't too late to witness the start of *Sea Shepherd*'s passage along the Panama Canal. Without this man-made short cut, linking Atlantic and Pacific, the ship would have had to keep on steaming for thousands more miles - right round Cape Horn.

A pilot came on board to supervise the jerky journey. There were stops in half a dozen giant locks, through which *Sea Shepherd* was pulled by four electric locomotives called 'mules'. So slow! Even Gary, watching each ship snail by, grew restless.

After nine hours and fifty miles, the canal trip ended at Balboa. Geoffrey Baggalley, having been defeated at dominoes by Peter Stokes for the umpteenth time, seized the opportunity to give the teenagers a lightning geography lesson. 'We are now entering the

Pacific Ocean,' he announced, '65 million square miles of it. The Atlantic is vast, but the Pacific' - he spread his arms - 'is by far the broadest and deepest of the world's oceans, bigger than all the land put together.'

Sea Shepherd pushed on into evening, then dawn, then another evening and another dawn. A smooth voyage which soothed away worries. Off Acapulco, Mexico, ever-observant Gary spotted a red seaplane that had crossed the ship's path several times since she left Panama. Now he remembered where he'd first seen the aircraft, or one like it: in Biscayne Bay, when *Sea Shepherd* arrived at Miami.

But soon the thought was wiped from his mind by the most astonishing spectacle. Luckily Susan, Norman, Vanessa, Yves and Ben Bellingham were there to share it with him. Out of the bright blue water, close to the ship, soared one...two...three immense creatures. Up and up. Like bats or birds grown to a phenomenal, freakish size. Twenty feet across.

'Manta-rays, also known as devil-fish,' Bellingham contributed, not hiding his elation. The mantas, each weighing 3,500 pounds-plus, belly-flopped into the waves with three foam-fountaining smacks.

'Why do they do that?' incredulous Susan asked.

'Nobody can really say,' Ben replied, 'but probably to get rid of parasites.'

After that, further wildlife sightings - flying fish and the Californian sea lions - seemed rather ordinary.

Susan felt sorry that Darren had missed the show, especially when she happened to see the scarlet-cheeked boy being told off by a furious Leslie Curtis. She liked the radio officer less and less.

The ship neared San Pedro - en route to helping the whales and sea otters.

Then, without warning, disaster struck. *Sea Shepherd* lost speed. Electronic equipment began to blink and break down. Captain Alexander hastened below from the bridge. He almost collided with the Chief Engineer stomping up from the engine-room. The engineer's face was streaked with sweat and grime, and veins stood

68

out on his forehead. 'Some swine has put sand in the oil. It'll ruin the engines, cripple the ship.'

Alexander clenched his fist...'Sabotage!'

6 Black death

Willed on by her crew and passengers, *Sea Shepherd* limped the last miles to San Pedro. In the juddering din deep below decks, the engineer let loose a stream of oaths and vowed vengeance. No torture was excruciating enough for whoever had harmed his precious machinery.

Captain Alexander's feelings were hardly more moderate, but he wore a cool mask as he issued clipped orders to the men around him on the bridge. Only his posture betrayed the boiling anger inside. Who did it? How? When? The questions pounded in his head. He needn't ask why. That was obvious - to scupper The Eden Mission.

With a slight pressure on the wheel, Alexander eased *Sea Shepherd* through the San Pedro Channel. The ship's engines made a rasping noise. An expert job of sabotage, the captain conceded bitterly. Done by somebody who knew where to cause most damage. Somebody who had access to the engine-room. Somebody on board at this moment.

An anchor clanked from the bow, broke the water and sank to find a firm hold on the ocean floor. Tugging tightly at her chain, *Sea Shepherd* came to rest off San Pedro, the port of Los Angeles.

Alexander's anger subsided; now dread took its place. Perhaps the engines were beyond repair, maybe the voyage - not half-completed - was over. Bracing himself for the worst, he strode unseeing to his cabin and a meeting with the engineer. *Sea Shepherd*'s fate was all that concerned him. Later he would decide the fate of the person, or people, who'd struck at her heart.

The youngsters, gossiping and gesticulating, assembled on deck. Was the rumoured sabotage true? Debate died down when Ben Bellingham approached. 'We've suffered a setback,' he said, 'a severe setback. But The Eden Mission continues - and you're part of it. So be ready to disembark in five minutes, as planned.'

Susan sighted a pert little boat rounding the harbour wall. The yellow launch swaggered towards them. *Sea Shepherd*'s gangway had been lowered to within a foot of the softly undulating water. A sailor tied the launch to the bottom of the gangway. Led by Bellingham and followed by Masterson and Baggalley, the six teenagers began their cautious descent to the boat. Susan grasped the rope handrail.

All aboard - without mishap. Gary winked at Susan and sat next to her in the stern. The launch grew friskier each moment, like a playful pony eager to be free. Then she was off, bucking to shore. Too short a ride for Gary's taste, but he realised they were not on a pleasure spree.

At San Pedro the party boarded a mini-bus which was soon speeding north to Santa Barbara - and the Marine Mammal Center.

The youngsters trooped out of the bus and into an impressive white building. Ben was bustled away by a secretary for a discussion with the center's top official. The rest of the party stood around. What now?

'Howdy, folks.' A man of about 30, with long hair and sporting a gaudy cowboy shirt, introduced himself. 'I'm Professor Kelsey... call me Joss. Please come this way.'

A professor, eh? He didn't fit Susan's idea of an egghead. If this was California style, she liked it. Vanessa evidently agreed, linking her arm through Susan's. The group gathered in a hall lined with photographs and diagrams. At one end lay a colossal skeleton - the length of two railway carriages.

Joss Kelsey spoke up: 'Mr. Bellingham will be back before long, which means I won't bore you with too many details about the center's work. Just to say that this place is devoted to the study and protection of marine mammals. From the largest to the smallest. From that guy there' - he pointed to the skeleton - 'the blue whale, to the pint-sized sea otter.'

Kelsey loped over and patted the bones affectionately. 'Mightiest creature God ever made, nothing to match it in the whole four-and-a-half-billion-year history of the world. And it's probably doomed to extinction. Thanks to a pushy newcomer known as homo sapiens, alias man. Whales have been roaming the oceans for 50 million years, whereas our ancestors hadn't learned to walk upright until a few hundred thousand years ago.'

The professor, noticing Darren's expression, tried to strike a cheerier note. 'The blue's heart is heavier than all of you put together, beats like a giant kettledrum and is the height of this gentleman' - he indicated Johnny Masterson. 'Hot blood is pumped around the whale's 170-ton bulk, along arteries so big that you' - Kelsey grinned at Darren - 'could've swum through them as a kid.

'Maybe, with a lotta luck, it *will* survive.'

If Kelsey needed encouragement to carry on, his audience provided plenty. The facts flowed. Among those lodging in Gary's mind was that a full-size blue whale can generate one thousand horsepower with its twenty-foot tail flukes. But when he heard that a baby blue increases in weight 30,000 million times during the first two years, Gary doubted his ears. Then Kelsey elaborated. Starting as a barely visible egg of 0.000035 ounces inside its mother, the calf is born nearly eleven months later. It measures 23 feet and weighs $2^{1}/_{2}$ tons. A year after that, it has expanded to a fifty-foot, 26-tonner - nourished for seven months on one-ton daily intakes of nutritious mother's milk. With this start, it may live to be 120.

Norman asked: 'Whales aren't as intelligent as humans, are they?'

Kelsey chuckled. 'Maybe they're brighter. When I think of some people I've met, that's not claiming much. For one thing, whales don't destroy their environment. For another, they co-operate with each other, even different species. Their brains are bigger than ours, particularly the parts associated with intelligence. The truth is these majestic leviathans are still something of a mystery.'

Susan caught the professor's attention. 'Joss, is the blue whale really doomed? Can't it make a come-back now hunters have promised to leave it in peace?'

Kelsey put his hands together. The blue's future is doubtful, he explained. Since the 1870s, war on whales has been waged from steamships armed with harpoon guns. In this century, all-out war was declared. Many species suffered horrendous casualties - and the blue, too big and swift for earlier whalers, became a prime target. The survivors were few and scattered. Could they find partners in the wide oceans? And if they did and mated successfully, would the cows' offspring - a single calf every two or three years - be enough to boost a population with an annual death rate from natural causes of four to eight per cent?

Kelsey added: 'Even without harpoons, man goes on stabbing the whale in the back. How? By turning its home into a dirty, poisonous place. Pollution...that's humanity's latest gift to marine creatures. A foul river of agricultural pesticides and herbicides, industrial chemicals, sewage and nuclear waste flows from the land into the sea - to circulate like bad news around the globe.'

But the worst curse off California's coast, said Kelsey, is oil. Not far from shore an ever-lengthening line of oil platforms marches along past scenery as beautiful as any on earth. Accidents happen. A minor oil spill is serious enough, 'as you'll soon see for yourselves. But a major blowout, a full-scale flood - it'd be ecologically devastating...'

A pause. Ben Bellingham had returned. He apologised for interrupting, and shook Kelsey's hand. Time to move on. Everyone thanked Joss and, with final farewells, the party filed out.

The mini-bus was waiting, engine ticking over. A brief trip through sunlit streets would end at a pier where a boat stood by to take the visitors sightseeing - sights they'd never want to see again.

*

Ninety-five miles to the south, beyond San Pedro harbour wall, *Sea Shepherd* floated at elegant ease; a fine vessel in first-class condition. Or so a casual observer might think.

After the Chief Engineer had delivered a damage report to Captain Alexander they toured the engine-room. It was still and silent. The men spoke quietly, as if in the presence of a sick friend. Only when they left did Alexander ask: 'What's your verdict, Chief? Any hope?'

The engineer looked like a doctor about to announce tragedy. Alexander stiffened his back. 'Not good, uh?'

'There's still a chance, Jim. A slim chance. Won't know till the engines are stripped down. Just possible they can be repaired - if we can get the spare parts. Otherwise the machinery might as well be scrap-metal.'

Little to celebrate, but enough to lighten Alexander's leaden spirits. 'Right, Chief, let's give it a go. We're not beaten yet.'

But the engineer didn't stir. Glowering, he muttered: 'If I ever get my hands on the scum that did this, God 'elp him!'

Alexander: 'Don't worry - I'll take care of the culprit. First things first, though. Our job now is to bring *Sea Shepherd* back to active life...'

Farther up the coast, the Santa Barbara launch continued her putt-putt-putting progress out to sea, leaving the pier behind in a paper-chase of foam. Gary and Susan huddled in the bow by Ben and a local naturalist. Scanning the horizon, Susan saw the smudged shapes of islands gradually sharpening into focus. Gary counted the nearer oil platforms, like tin Titans wading in the water.

'Eleven,' commented the naturalist. 'Quite awe-inspiring in their way, aren't they? From shore, all lit up at night, they look pretty. Remind me of Christmas trees.'

This was his only favourable remark about the platforms. He disapproved of contraptions that could go wrong and spew black death into the ocean.

Animals were what excited him - such as the whales which

74

paraded in frolicking convoys past the windows of his beach-side house each Christmas. Grey whales, forty-foot migrants from the frozen north, make a 12,000-mile round trip to winter off Lower California where cows give birth to their calves in warm and shallow lagoons.

'Year after year they return. It's always a thrill.'

His gaze clouded and he gestured contemptuously at a nearby oil platform. 'Spills can choke a whale. This applies particularly to baleen whales - the blue and the grey, for instance. They feed by filtering water through their baleen, a hanging fringe of a substance similar to fingernails, and licking off the trapped plankton. If the filter is clogged the whale starves.'

Gary, Susan and the others sat in wordless contemplation, scarcely aware of the island until the boat bumped ashore.

The naturalist led them over grass-tufted sand to a calm cove, the perfect picnicking place. But not today. Not since oil had stained and smeared the beach. And who wanted to picnic beside two dead bodies?

A grey whale and her calf, pecked at by birds, were already rotting. Susan's tears welled. The calf, though at least twelve feet long, looked fragile and pathetic. It seemed to be cuddling up to its mother. Both were coated in glutinous oil.

Gary squeezed Susan's arm, but he could no more comfort her than he could the lifeless carcasses. The cow's slightly curved mouth suggested a sad smile.

Trying not to tread in the oil, Gary, Susan, Darren, Vanessa, Yves and Norman shuffled past the beached whales. Bellingham, Masterson, Baggalley and the naturalist tagged on behind. A procession of mourners paying their last respects.

No one regretted being aboard the launch again, bound for Santa Barbara. After a while the naturalist observed: 'That cow and her calf should've migrated north weeks ago, like the other greys...' He broke off, then resumed: 'S'pose we should be grateful the oil's out of range of the sea otters - so far.'

On the bus to San Pedro, the students made mumbled conversation

75

or napped. An exhausting day. It was night when they mounted *Sea Shepherd*'s gangway. Appetites were keen, but dinner just wasn't the same without Ben, Johnny Masterson and Alexander - all engaged in a conference about the battered engines.

After the meal the youngsters ambled to their cabins, too tired to talk. They would need to be fresh for tomorrow.

As if by arrangement, Gary and Susan both rose extra early and emerged into the corridor at almost the same moment. Such 'coincidences' no longer surprised them.

They walked the deck. A gilt-edged mist was playing tricks with the sea view, gull-noisy, veiling and unveiling ships and buoys.

'Will you miss me, Gary?' Susan's head was turned away.

'Er...yes. 'Course I will.'

'Really?'

'Really!'

Susan hugged him. 'Wish you were coming too.'

'I know,' said Gary. 'But it's only for a few days.'

'You will miss me though?'

'Very much, stupid.'

Reassured, Susan could now do full justice to her breakfast. The mood among the young passengers at the captain's table was a curious mixture: good-humoured and gloomy. Soon the group would be divided. Yves obviously didn't like the prospect of parting from Vanessa, any more than Susan wanted to leave Gary. But The Eden Mission, as Ben frequently repeated, must go on.

Susan, Vanessa and Darren went below to collect their luggage. Masterson already had his beside him. Effortlessly he swung the kit bag over his shoulder and strolled out on deck. He peered through the mist, a blanket slowly tearing into bigger and bigger holes. Masterson discerned the approaching shuttle boat.

Without looking round, he sensed the presence of the three teenagers. What was delaying the fifth member of the shore party - Stokes? Masterson's brows knit. A real tough guy, Susan thought. Just as well he's on our side.

By now the launch beneath was fidgeting at her moorings. Still no Stokes. Ben Bellingham sent a sailor to find the tardy teacher, and eventually the man returned with an apologetic Stokes. 'So sorry, didn't mean to hold you up. I seem to have mislaid my pocket calculator. Always take it with me...'

Vanessa sighed sympathetically as the maths master shifted from foot to foot. Masterson showed less understanding. 'Perhaps we can get going - if everyone's *ready*.'

Captain Alexander, Bellingham and the trio of youngsters who were staying behind said goodbye and good luck to the departing group. Also present was Curtis, his grin as phoney as ever. Susan noted the cold hard stare he gave Darren.

Gary kept waving until the boat edged round the harbour wall and out of sight. Susan would be back in no time, he told himself. Meanwhile the shipboard contingent had plenty to do.

There was a different driver at the wheel of the mini-bus, young and fair haired. Vanessa adopted a provocative pose, which Susan ruined by shoving her forward. The shore party settled down for a longish journey. North to Monterey, where surf-riding sea otters play off the coast.

The bus moved briskly through the Hollywood district of Los Angeles. Vanessa put on a film star act - for the benefit of the driver and Johnny Masterson. Susan watched, half amused, half irritated. In the rear seat pasty-faced Darren crouched with a hold-all clutched to his chest. Across the aisle Peter Stokes emptied his pockets. Searching for the calculator?

As the bus passed beyond the city limits, Susan got up to stretch her legs. She lurched towards the rear and, apparently by accident, flopped beside Darren. 'Mind if I sit here?' He didn't actually object, so she stayed.

Which was his favourite animal...did he like the food on *Sea Shepherd*...and what of the sabotage?

His answers were short, as grudgingly given as those of a prisoner under interrogation. But Susan persisted, determined to make friends.

77

Little by little the boy dropped his defences. It occurred to Susan that being on your guard all the time must be very tiring. Tentatively she asked about Curtis, wondering how Darren had become acquainted with him and what sort of person he was.

Darren raised his defences double quick. 'Dunno what you mean. He's nothing to me. Just another big-head officer!'

Susan was sorry she'd mentioned Curtis. A mistake. She changed the subject - to herself, her school, hobbies, family. Darren relaxed; he even laughed at something Susan said.

'What are *your* parents like?' she inquired.

Darren hesitated. 'Don't see much of my father - he's away a lot. But my mother...she's great. I've got a picture.' He undid his bag, felt inside and pulled out a perspex photograph holder. 'That's Mum.' He handed it to Susan.

'Nice,' she murmured. 'You look alike.'

This seemed to please him.

The bus wheels whirred, carrying the five ever closer to Monterey and the sea otters. Stokes had nodded off, and Vanessa continued to flirt energetically. Susan sat back by Darren in companionable silence.

Santa Barbara's outskirts. Hillside houses, red-roofed, craned over each other's shoulders to get a better view of a too-blue-to-be-true bay below. On her first visit, Susan's mind was full of whales and so she had been blinded to the splendour of this lovely coastal town.

Lunch loomed - and before many more miles, the bus drew up at a diner. The party poured out. Everybody was empty-handed, except Darren. He insisted on taking his hold-all.

Susan downed a pizza, ice-cream and Coke as if competing against the clock, then had to wait for the others. They appeared to her to be chewing each mouthful with cow-like deliberation. Vanessa, predictably, was last to finish. Soon after, Stokes paid the bill.

On the bus, Susan chatted again to Darren. Now his frosty manner had thawed he was almost fun. Time and the landscape

78

flitted by, and as the offshore oil platforms fell farther and farther behind so did the memory of them. Susan and Darren ran out of things to say, but there was no awkwardness between the two.

Susan thought she would write a postcard to her parents - she'd been putting it off - and foraged in her bag for a ballpoint. She wished she had packed properly instead of just throwing stuff in.

'Darren, have you got something I can write with?'

He produced a pen from his hold-all.

'Thanks,' said Susan. 'Hmmm...must've cost a bit. I'll be careful with it.'

A sort of wariness crossed the boy's face, a reluctance to look at her. Shy suddenly? Susan understood that problem from personal experience. She stared out the window, seeking words to begin the postcard. Ten minutes later she gave back the pen. Darren had become a stranger, stiff and spiky as an icicle. Susan tried and failed to restore their earlier intimacy. Had she said or done anything to upset him? He offered no clue. Sulk if you want, she thought. See if I care.

Huffily Susan reached for her book - you knew where you were with sea otters.

Very soon she *was* one, a furry sleeper adrift on her back in the rocking cradle of the ocean. Snoring gently, arms folded. Hardly waking, she covered her eyes with her paws. Pity about the sun's dazzle, but who could doze for long when there were games to play? She paddled towards the sound of chortling, cooing, whistling. Otters of all ages bent on sheer enjoyment. Joining in a game of catch, she tossed an empty shell to and fro. And when she tired of that she would play tug-of-war until the seaweed 'rope' snapped, or hide-and-seek among the kelp beds where otter food is found. Food. She dived, came up with a flat stone and some mussels in a pouch under her arm. Rolling over, she laid the stone on her chest and hammered the shell against the hard surface. *Rat-a-tat-tat*. Every mussel was broken open and eaten. She cleaned the scraps from her fur - rinsed it, scrubbed it, smoothed it. For though she was a water creature, water must never touch her skin. She had seen what happened to otters when their coats became matted. The chilly sea killed them. Another snooze...

Susan the otter abruptly resumed human form as the bus horn hooted at some motorist. A sideways glance confirmed that Darren was still doing his imitation of a sulky statue. Back to the book. Sea otters' coats are made up of 800 million hairs. The warmest and, many people think, the handsomest fur in the world. No wonder the poor things came within a hair's breadth of being hunted out of existence. But for a last-minute truce, they wouldn't be around now, splashing and bobbing in the shallows. Susan closed the book.

Twisting in her seat, she peeked out the rear window. A maroon pick-up truck was just rounding the curve behind them. It had been there when she last looked - hours ago. Susan shivered. A spasm of anxiety. Why? The Sea World thug? Nerves, jumpy. She shook her head. Don't be daft, Susan. But the spooky feeling, a sense of being pursued, wouldn't leave her.

'Johnny!'

Masterson abandoned the driver to Vanessa's undivided attention and swayed to the back of the bus. 'Your humble servant, ma'm.' His jaunty air vanished at the sight of Susan's distress. 'What's up?' She blurted her fears. Masterson watched the truck for the next few miles.

Then it turned off at a side-road. Susan was contrite. But Masterson thanked her for alerting him. 'It's better to be safe than sorry.'

Highway One hugs California's coast, giving a grandstand view of the pounding Pacific, a bird's-eye view of birds such as the cormorants airing wet wings on the rocks or scudding the wave crests in a never-finished quest for fish.

Journey's end was near, nearer still. Bald-headed mountains cooled their feet in the sea. The bus seemed desperate to swallow the remaining road. Monterey. Hooray!

Some 350 miles away, Ben Bellingham rose from a padded leather chair in a Los Angeles television studio. The interview had gone well. Despite the hostility of one or two reporters who criticised him for minding other people's business - just like you, he was tempted to say - Bellingham had broadcast his conservation appeal loud and clear.

Gary, Norman and Yves also participated. Treated more kindly, they were asked what The Eden Mission meant to them.

Cameras clicked as Bellingham and the boys made for the studio exit. 'We certainly told 'em, didn't we?' Ben twinkled.

In the taxi to San Pedro, Gary mused happily. Susan'll be green with envy.

Aboard *Sea Shepherd*...encouraging developments. Marine mechanics from Long Beach, in consultation with the Chief Engineer, had broken good news: the engines were not a write-off, could be revived. Work was already under way. Meanwhile the ship's midget submarines nosed out to explore, and further research projects went ahead on schedule.

Dinner proved a jollier meal than expected. *Sea Shepherd*'s company retired to a comparatively untroubled sleep.

But in the small-hours of the morning, a nightmare that had haunted California's conservationists for years came horribly true. A drilling rig exploded, then an oil platform. Several men died instantly, while the gushing black tide slurped onwards.

Up north, in Monterey, breakfast TV and radio bulletins trumpeted the first headlines of death and destruction. The full story would emerge later. But no one could foresee the dire drama to come.

Unaware of events, Susan and the rest of the group set out from their lodgings at eight o'clock. They reached the wharf; now to find *Lutris*. Masterson asked for directions. A sour-faced fisherman jerked his thumb at a cruiser a few berths away. Johnny thanked him. The man slouched off, saying nothing. 'Have a nice day,' Susan called, not quite meaning it.

Lutris, with flaking white paint, was probably the shabbiest craft on the wharf. Her owners - husband-and-wife biologists - couldn't afford to spend money on anything but the necessities of their work. Susan saw, fluttering from the stern, an orange pennant which proclaimed FRIENDS OF THE SEA OTTER.

'Hi there!' The big voice matched the figure at the top of the gangway. Even Johnny Masterson had to crick his neck. 'Name's Hank,' rumbled the straw-headed, ruddy-cheeked giant. 'Come on up.' Vanessa skipped forward to lead the climbing column.

Hank pumped each hand in turn, going easy on a grip that could be numbing. 'This is Rhonda, my wife.' A petite and vivacious woman, as brown as a nut, warmly welcomed them. Beside Hank she appeared tinier still. From the look in Darren's eyes, Susan could tell that Rhonda had won his heart immediately.

Soon *Lutris* was butting the waves beyond Monterey. The contrast between their hospitable hosts and the grouchy fishermen on the quay caused Stokes to mention the man's attitude. Hank expressed no surprise. '*We're* the sea otter's friends, but a lot of fishermen aren't. They'd kill every last one if they could. You see, shellfish are in short supply - and otters get the blame. Wrongly, I think.'

Rhonda ushered the teenagers to the side of the cruiser. Her bronzed arm rested lightly on Darren's shoulder. 'Use your binoculars,' she advised. Vanessa spied the otter first. 'Oooh... sweet! He's half out of the water, standing up. And look, he's shading his eyes with his paw...like a sailor staring across the sea.' Then Darren and Susan spotted two more of the chocolate-coloured creatures, which clung to each other tightly. 'Pups,' Rhonda explained. 'They're scared because they don't trust us, yet. The adults get nervous too, and they vary in temperament; some are bold, some bashful. A bit like human beings.' Darren met her gentle gaze.

Cutting the engine, Hank waited for *Lutris* to lose momentum, then lowered a mooring buoy. He and Rhonda boarded a rubber dinghy. 'Room for three passengers,' he said. Vanessa and Darren followed Susan down, steadied by Rhonda. Hank started to row.

'Rafts' of otters to right and left. Rhonda pointed out a pup wrapped in strands of kelp. 'That's to stop it drifting off,' she whispered. 'It can float but not swim. So when Ma goes for food she ties the baby up.' Nearby, a four-foot female lay back and suckled her new offspring in a loving embrace. Another mother patiently coaxed an older pup to make its first swimming movements. A third, combing with cat-like claws, groomed her baby, deaf to its waaah-waaahing protests.

Hank scooped something from the bottom of the dinghy - a cooked crab - and slipped smoothly overboard. Lolling on the water, otter-fashion, he began to tuck in to the crab. Before long, an inquisitive male approached. He studied Hank. An imploring paw reached out. Hank passed a piece of crab - and, side by side, man and otter enjoyed a floating snack.

Over years, Hank and Rhonda had forged an extraordinary bond with otters. The teenagers felt privileged to be included.

Returning to *Lutris* was like being dragged away from a fair. On board, Darren plied Rhonda with questions. Susan had never seen him so enthusiastic. She listened in. Sea otters, said Rhonda, were once common - from Japan to Mexico. But the fur trade altered that. Even today, under protection, they occupy only one-fifth of their original territory.

Otters, unlike other sea mammals, have no layer of fat to insulate them, relying instead on their coats...and lots of food. They relish abalone - outsize salt-water snails. Unfortunately restaurant-goers also drool over this delicacy. 'Which is why the fishermen get mad,' Rhonda concluded.

But Darren wouldn't let her go. She laughed. 'We'll talk again, maybe tomorrow. Meantime I'm proud to enrol you as one of the Friends of the Sea Otter.'

Down south, there was no such leisurely pleasure for ecologists. Oil had overwhelmed the ocean around Santa Barbara's platforms. From a patrol boat Ben Bellingham tracked the darkly heaving invasion. The anti-pollution squads, locked in combat with a superior and ever-strengthening foe, were being beaten back.

Bellingham brooded on the carnage among fish and birds. A single consolation: the south-flowing current should sweep the oil far from shore - and from the otters. Unless the wind changed direction...

7 Jinxed

Sea Shepherd was making a rapid recovery. At first her crew had rejoiced that she would not be permanently paralysed. Then the feeling turned into something else - suspicion. It infected the ship from bow to stern, from bridge to engine-room, like an epidemic. Nobody trusted anybody. Even close comrades became uneasy with each other, unnaturally secretive. And tempers were fraying. The saboteur must be rooted out. The sooner the better.

'Bloody maniac! Get away! Get awaaay!' Ben Bellingham yelled, arms flailing. He knew it was useless, but... Seconds later, a shuddering crunch. The sky tilted crazily. He was flung headlong, the breath knocked from his lungs. The patrol boat's wooden hull split and splintered, axed almost in two by the prow of a trawler.

Bellingham heard faint groans. Of the shocked, injured, dying? He couldn't tell. Wrestling with giddiness, he somehow managed to stand. His fuzzy vision cleared. Chaos. Three or four of his companions - catapulted overboard - were floundering in oil, groping for bits of wreckage. Another figure floated face down. The remains of their craft sank beneath Bellingham's feet.

Swimming slowly, he took care not to swallow the poisonous black water. Bellingham caught sight of the trawler. She showed no sign of stopping, was blundering on as though nothing had happened! Around him the distressed men and women, some barely conscious, tried to stay afloat. A few were coughing up oil. For them, he feared, help would come too late. If it came at all.

Someone shouted. Bellingham searched in every direction - and saw... Yes. Thank God! A coastguard cutter rip-roaring to the rescue at maximum revs.

On the cutter, hastily converted into a casualty station, Ben did what he could to aid his colleagues: giving artificial respiration, applying bandages, comforting the delirious. He was one of the lucky ones, escaping with only cuts and bruises. He felt strangely guilty. But other emotions rocked him too. Rage and a momentary desire for revenge. What a mess!

Eleven people - eight men, three women - had departed by patrol boat from Santa Barbara. The same number was returning. This time, though, two were dead and at least another three gravely ill. The sound of retching reminded Bellingham that oil might yet cause further fatalities.

How had the trawler come to hit the boat? Was the skipper insane? Drunk? Blind? And why hadn't the ship picked up survivors? The chief coastguard reeled off these queries, not expecting answers.

Ben Bellingham: 'I'm beginning to think the ramming was deliberate.'

The coastguard mulled over the possibility.

Elsewhere on the cutter, an officer had radioed emergency services to stand by and alerted law-enforcement vessels to detain the rogue ship.

He tried to contact the trawler. A fruitless exercise.

The trawler skipper stood stock-still, as if in a trance, and steered for the shore. He looked neither to right nor left, didn't speak, didn't twitch a muscle. The knife at his throat had transformed him into a submissive zombie. Beside him dangled the innards of the radio, like the entrails of a disembowelled animal, rendering the ship deaf and dumb. The man with the knife had sworn to do worse to the skipper if opposed. All on board believed him. So, powerless to prevent it, they'd allowed the trawler to be hijacked and used as a battering-ram.

Though literally scared stiff, the skipper could still think. He recalled the moment of impact and the hoarse utterance of his captor: 'Adios, Bellingham! Adios!' What did he mean? Who was this psychopath, this ugly stowaway who had plucked a knife from his boot? As long as he lived, the skipper would remember the man's face - scarred, with eyes that glittered like the knife...

The point pressed into his throat. 'We land soon,' the hated voice told him in an accent that was either Spanish or South American. 'Be ready. Any tricks - I kill you.'

When the trawler ran aground, two figures clambered down a rope-ladder - hijacker and hostage - watched by sailors who wondered whether they would ever see their skipper again. Dead or alive.

Aching, worn out and depressed, Ben Bellingham trudged up *Sea Shepherd*'s gangway. He needed a drink and a friend to share his troubles with. Curtis drifted into view, not a person Bellingham chose to confide in. He nodded at the radio officer and set course for the captain's cabin.

James Alexander, elbows on his desk, chin cupped in his hands, squinted irritably. Bellingham waited for the captain to say hello. He didn't. His grey hair, sleekly brushed on other occasions, was dishevelled. What do *you* want? The words weren't spoken, but Ben could hear them just the same.

Uninvited, he sat opposite Alexander. 'Nice to be back, Jim,' he said, a shade ironically. 'You've obviously been having as much fun as I have.' With belated good manners Alexander held out his hand. Soon Bellingham was reliving the trawler incident and its deadly aftermath. To his surprise, then annoyance, he found the captain indifferent.

'Must catch the saboteur,' Alexander muttered. 'And one of our submarines is overdue. I've notified the maritime authorities. Should've returned four hours ago...'

Bellingham left the cabin, more downcast than when he'd entered. Just as well the youngsters were away. He thought of the Monterey party and of the three boys - Gary, Norman and Yves - touring schools in Southern California to talk about The Eden Mission. The Eden Mission! Bellingham sighed.

For an update on the global front, he dropped in to *Sea Shepherd*'s data-processing centre. The experience did not hearten him. Among other things, he learned that police investigating the Bahamas spear gun attack had drawn a blank - as blank as the ecologists' film. Odd, Bellingham mused. He was growing accustomed to the inexplicable.

Dejectedly he descended to his cabin and his bunk. Sleep, Ben, sleep. He pulled off his boots, grunting with the effort. 'Tired,' he murmured, and fell back on the so-soft pillow. But he was not cushioned against memories. Shattering timbers, moans of the shipwrecked, reek of the tainted sea...could he ever forget? The bereaved families - how many more before the night was through? Sleep, Ben. No chance. The trawler had him in a net.

Next morning, hardly rested, Bellingham forced himself upright. Perhaps today held happier events.

'The sub is still missing.' Alexander squeezed past him in the corridor. 'Navy's doing what it can.' Bellingham lost all appetite for breakfast. He plodded up to the deck, thinking what he had not dared admit to himself till now: The Eden Mission is jinxed. Oh for better news!

Within minutes his wish was granted. A radio operator told him that the tide was turning in the oil battle. Fire-fighters had extinguished the blaze on the bent and blackened platform, and the process of 'capping' the pipes had begun. A cement and water mixture was being pumped down to seal off the erupting source.

Ben Bellingham gripped the operator's arm, grateful for even this partial reprieve from despair. But his new optimism did not last. Before long, the same man who'd lifted Ben's hopes dashed them by delivering another message. A message that chilled him to the bone. The wind had freshened, veered, reversed the current, and was thrusting the foul slick towards the beaches. Towards the sea otters.

South of Monterey the cruiser *Lutris* sploshed past playing otters, through waves flecked with fizzy foam like lemonade. Susan's throat was dry. She had been looking too long and hard for tarry streaks, first marks of the oil that advanced inexorably beyond the horizon. Darren and Vanessa shared the anxious sentry duty.

In the cockpit behind them, Hank and his wife Rhonda prepared for a grade one emergency. Masterson and Stokes tried not to get in the way and awaited instructions as to what - if anything - they could do.

Hank lumbered forward to join the youngsters. He seemed stooped from carrying a heavy burden.

Susan bit her lip. 'The oil will finish them, won't it?'

'No.' Hank was determined. 'We're not gonna let that happen.'

'How can you stop it?' Darren spoke for the other two.

Hank hesitated... 'Those boats over there belong to the US Fish and Wildlife Service. They're well equipped and can transmit sounds to lure the otters closer or, in our case, drive them away. We'll move as many as we can out of danger.'

Vanessa expressed scepticism.

'It's a fact,' Hank insisted. 'The sound of a killer whale will make otters flee, and a bawling pup will bring adults hurrying to tend it.'

But Susan found no solace. The oil was bound to get some of them, then what? They'd have to be caught, drugged and kept in captivity. An inevitable process if they were to be cleaned and released where the sea was safe.

Susan dangled her hand over the side. 'Hank...my book says otters are very sensitive and mope when they have to leave their home or are separated from their families. They can die of stress.

Is that right?'

Hank cleared his throat. 'Er...yes, Susan. 'Fraid so. Let's look on the bright side though. Maybe the wind'll shift.'

Near Santa Barbara, a million slimy fingers were feeling for the shore. Appalled residents watched the fingers stretch and take hold, as if to haul the whole huge body of oil up and over the sand inch by inch until not a glint of gold showed through. And the stench!

An elderly, weather-beaten man shook his fist and said to those within earshot: 'I've seen a spill one-tenth the size of this pollute a thousand square miles of ocean and bury a hundred miles of holiday beaches in gluey muck a foot thick.'

Nobody responded - there was nothing to say.

Offshore the clean-up campaign was being conducted with frantic energy. Aircraft skimmed the sea surface, showering detergent. Abreast greasy waves, ships waged their own war. Some sprayed chemicals while towing a series of paddles. This broke the oil into droplets so that bacteria could 'eat' it easily. Elsewhere, vessels encircled the oil with floating booms and sucked it aboard.

On land, truck-loads of detergent had been dispatched to besieged beaches. There, fire-engines pumped out countless gallons of the milky liquid, then 'shampooed' the sand by hosing it with water. Meanwhile farm machinery ploughed up oil that had penetrated deep.

Throughout the days and floodlit nights to come, army, navy, air force and civilian personnel would keep up the fight against the wind-whipped slick. Could they win? They must.

Lutris was just one of a widely spaced flotilla of boats 'riding herd' on the otters along 230 miles of California's coastline. Assignment: to woo and shoo the creatures away to a secure place.

'It's for your own good,' Susan said to the bemused bewhiskered faces of two otters that *Lutris* approached.

90

This was going to be even harder than she thought, as Hank already knew. He also knew that the oil, once it invaded otter country, could complete the annihilation begun by fur traders in the early 1700s. No more Californian sea otters.

He checked the radio reports. All too soon the water on every side would grow a scummy skin.

Bellingham felt as though he had been on the wrong end of an uppercut.

'Right now, Ben, I don't give a damn about the otters. I've got other priorities. Like a lost submarine, and some Judas who's trying to disable my ship.'

Again Bellingham attempted to reason with Alexander. But the captain was in no mood for compromise. 'I can't spare key men like Grant and Masterson. I want them and the kids back on *Sea Shepherd*. By tomorrow - at the latest.'

Ben raised a placating palm. 'OK, OK. Calm down, Jim. Our enemies would love to see us falling out. We're on the same side, remember?'

Alexander exhaled slowly. 'You're right, of course. I apologise. Meant what I said, though, about recalling the groups.'

With considerable restraint Bellingham closed the captain's door gently. He climbed to the deck, hoping fresh air would cure his headache.

Less than 48 hours later the ship was weighing anchor off San Pedro. Much had occurred in that time, including the reluctant return of the students. Cutting short their schools tour, Gary, Norman and Yves were the first to arrive, accompanied by Philip Grant, Geoffrey Baggalley and Maude Mimpriss. Not long after, Johnny Masterson and Peter Stokes led in Susan, Vanessa and Darren.

The reunited companions joked with each other, but the jokes were feeble and the laughter was hollow. Everyone felt a sense of failure at a project abandoned half-way through.

Ben Bellingham made a final trip ashore - to visit the still sick survivors of the ramming. Next, in court, he listened to the testimony of the hijacked trawler crew. Disbelief surrendered to sympathy for the abducted skipper whose throat might by now have been slit.

Boarding *Sea Shepherd*, Bellingham was informed of Alexander's decision to leave without the two-man sub. The US navy would continue its search. In the corridor, Susan blocked his path, fixing him with watery eyes. The otters! He offered a few weak words and concluded: 'We'll just have to pray.'

So, in brilliant sunshine but under a shadow, the ship sailed. The promise of seeing and exploring the wonders of the Amazon should have stirred the blood. Instead it seemed like a dreary duty.

By mid-morning, however, the wind had faded to a whisper. Which meant... Susan hopped up and down. Which meant the current would reassert itself and carry the oil away from the otters.

A prayer answered? Susan was convinced of it. She wanted to run to Ben; but when she spotted him with Captain Alexander, both scowling, her happiness deflated like a leaking balloon. The shipboard atmosphere, tense and edgy, spoilt everything.

She latched on to Vanessa and the pair walked and talked listlessly. 'What's the time?' Vanessa asked after examining a bare wrist. Susan told her. 'Still can't get used to not having a watch,' Vanessa complained.

Susan paused at the rail, pensive. 'I wonder if it *was* stolen... Did Yves find his pen?' 'No. Don't think so.' Vanessa scuffed the deck. They moved on.

Some way off, by the bow, they identified the sulky silhouette of Darren. The person they had begun to get to know during the Monterey expedition might never have existed. Since setting foot again on *Sea Shepherd*, Darren had reverted to sullen silence. Susan didn't blame him - there was little enough joy around - but she did blame something, or rather someone, else. Curtis. Who at this moment seemed to have Darren cornered.

As the girls drew nearer they overheard the radio officer comment: 'Like father, like son, eh?' It had the stinging feel of a taunt. Noticing them suddenly, Darren reddened. He needed no further excuse to detach himself from Curtis.

In his cabin, Alexander rose and subjected each of the three listeners to intense scrutiny. 'So you see, gentlemen, the traitor is ever present. You may pass him a dozen times a day, eat with him, regard him as a friend. Could be anybody - even one of *us*.'

This was too much for Philip Grant. 'You're not suggesting...' Alexander waved him aside. 'No, Phil. I'm assuming you, Ben and Mr. Masterson are as innocent as I am. Just wanted to make the point that there's no shortage of suspects. I'll start going through the list with Mr. Masterson. Lousy job. But we've got to get him. Keep your wits about you.'

Vanessa parted from Susan, bored by the restless rambling, and left the younger girl alone with her thoughts - disturbing thoughts. Susan wished she could throw them overboard. Head down, mind threshing, she bumped into Yves. He was in a daydream. 'Sorry,' both said simultaneously. They chatted for a bit.

'Not found your pen, Yves?'

'Nope...How do you know about that?'

'Vanessa told me.'

'Ah, Vanessa.' Yves savoured the name in the way Susan reserved for her favourite food.

'What sort of pen was it?'

'Why? Have you seen it?'

'I can't say if you don't describe it!'

'Well, it's red - wine-coloured - with a gold top and a clip shaped like an arrow,' Yves recited. 'Does that ring a bell?'

'I'll go on looking, Yves. 'Bye for now.'

As he slouched off, Susan resisted the urge to call him back. She was tempted to tell him that she *had* seen his pen, or its twin, but she couldn't. Not yet. Not until she'd talked things over with Gary.

Gary and Susan rendezvoused after lunch, behind some lifeboats. In one helter-skeltering sentence she recounted how Darren had lent her a pen - *the* pen? - on the bus to Monterey; how she had remarked upon it; and how Darren had soon become curiously cold. That

93

abrupt switch in behaviour would make sense if - if he was a thief who feared being found out...

'Did you hear me?' Susan's tone suggested a stamped foot.

But Gary refused to be rushed into replying. Several more seconds elapsed, then: 'You were right to keep this to yourself. Could be a coincidence. And there's no *proof*.'

'So you don't think Darren stole the pen?'

'I didn't say that.'

'What about Vanessa's watch?'

'You're just guessing, Susan. I wouldn't be willing to sneak on somebody unless I was really sure, and you despise sneaks as much as I do.'

'A fat lot of help *you* are!' Susan retorted, but secretly she agreed with Gary.

Gradually, day by day, all succumbed to the steady rhythm of an ocean voyage. Meals, lessons, lectures...it was as if the youngsters had experienced no other life.

The hours hung heavy sometimes. One afternoon Susan nagged and wheedled Norman into displaying his conjuring skills. Yves, Gary, Vanessa and Susan squatted on deck-chairs and the impromptu show commenced. Shy Norman became a wizard. He was good, very good, brilliant. Vanessa *aaahed* as he flipped and shuffled cards like a gambler in a Western. Then he magicked a coin from behind her ear.

Seeing Darren pass by in the background, Yves got up and went over to him. 'Come and watch - it's great.' But Darren shook his head. Yves retraced his steps. 'What a room-mate! For months I've tried to be friendly. Let him rot...'

Shoulders hunched, Darren traversed the deck, an apparently aimless figure. Aimless? He was far from that. He had an aim, a single aim: to get even with Curtis.

The radio room was always unmanned at this time. Still, he must be extra careful. Too many prying officers around lately. His senses, keen as a cat's, served him well. Only a few more yards. Darren twisted the door handle and slipped inside.

Curtis's jacket hung over the back of a chair. Darren worked quickly, rifling the pockets. Comb, diary, chewing-gum. Nothing worth having. Wait. A lighter, engraved with the initials 'L.C.'. That'll do. He tested it with a flick. The yellow jet surged, shot upwards, singeing his hair. And a wall-chart was on fire! Desperately he grabbed the jacket and beat out the flames. Tearing the charred corner from the chart, he dumped it in a waste-paper bin, then made his getaway with the lighter.

As Darren shut the door behind him, the paper in the bin glowed - breathed on by a breeze through the porthole.

Fifteen minutes later, an alarm sounded on the bridge. Water-sprinklers, triggered by heat, had been set off. Where? First Officer Philip Grant scanned the panel, found the flashing light. 'Fire squad to the radio room.' Loud-speakers relayed his instruction.

Kicking open the door, the men were engulfed in a searing acrid fog. Behind it smouldered the remnants of God-knows-what. 'Masks on, bring extinguishers!' Frothing foam obliterated the last embers, and the fire combatants emerged sooty faced.

'What a bloody shambles!' Leslie Curtis amidst the sodden ruins - melted wires, discoloured metal, blistered paint - of his once orderly empire.

'I agree, *Mister* Curtis.' Captain Alexander's voice was sword-sharp. 'Find out if the radio can be salvaged. After that we'll go into the little matter of how this happened...'

Alexander turned on his heel and marched away to conduct a series of meetings that would threaten to equal the fire in temperature.

Meanwhile Maude Mimpriss's lesson on medieval English poetry was failing to fascinate her pupils. Only later did they hear of the blaze, and, perhaps because mishaps had become almost common, reacted with comparative calm. Except Darren. His features, Susan noticed, fleetingly registered - shock.

95

8 Hannah

Susan and Gary mounted the companionway for their twice-round-the-deck evening walk. As usual Susan was doing most of the talking. Gary, slightly behind her and not paying full attention, took several seconds to realise that the words had stuck in her throat. Then he knew why: the high and wide heavens were flushed crimson, pink, orange. Susan imagined all the skies of the world draining through ruby rivers to flood this one sky. Even by Caribbean standards it was an exceptional sunset.

They were not the only spectators on deck. The most unexpected people, seasoned mariners among them, had halted in mid-stride to stare. Gary's gaze shifted to the water - like everything else, that too seemed peculiarly altered. Its glossy surface reminded him of newly cut coal, or the rubbery skin of a sea lion.

From the bridge window, Captain Alexander regarded the sky more with wariness than wonder. Smeared blood was what he saw. Why so morbid? Absurd. The strain of command must be getting to him. No, it wasn't. Think. What had he forgotten, what warning was trying to break through the other layers of worry?

Alexander went off duty. At his cabin desk he thumbed the pages of the ship's log. A catalogue of misfortunes that an average seafarer might not meet in a lifetime. The fire was merely the latest blow. Alexander began to write. After half an hour he pushed the book aside. Undressing, he thought without sympathy of Curtis and his assistants labouring to resurrect the radio.

Around midnight a rating on the bridge took a routine barometer reading. The pressure was low, ominously low, and falling. He reported to Philip Grant. The first officer stiffened. Storm brewing. When the placid Caribbean lost its temper, no safe shelter could be found.

Before long *Sea Shepherd* started to rumba, wiggling her backside, wagging her head. Grant gave orders to extend the stabilisers, and two underwater 'wings' slid out from the hull.

Below decks, Susan didn't need a barometer to predict dirty weather. She had got the message early and, while Vanessa fussed, was heaving into the sink.

Incredulously Grant traced the plummeting pressure - he'd never seen such a sustained dive. A rain-filled gust struck the window, like a giant paw cuffing with claws bared, and the wind sobbed as if in sorrow at what it was destined to do. Is the ship secure? Grant sent a patrol party to ensure all hatches were sealed and portholes covered. *Sea Shepherd*'s rumba changed tempo. The roller-coaster ride was under way.

An experienced sailor, Philip Grant was not prone to panic. But his mouth had a sour taste, the taste of dread. He was bombarded by images of the ocean in outright rebellion - not real-life gales he had passed through, but illustrations of *tempests* from boyhood books. Though he busied himself with work, another vision possessed him: a snowy-maned wave rearing a hundred feet, astern, in the moonlight, to avalanche on a trapped vessel. It had happened once to a tanker in the Pacific.

Sea Shepherd climbed up and tobogganed down steepening slopes. Grant blinked as lightning fractured the sky, briefly illuminating a near and a far ferment of water. The waiting waves. Twenty-footers. Grant noted the wind speed - 50 m.p.h. - and rang the engine-room.

In the galley, piled plates teetered, tumbled and smashed to pieces. In the cabins hardly anybody slept. A solicitous Gary was helping Norman to his feet after he'd been tipped out of the top bunk; Vanessa was escorting Susan on her fifth visit to the bathroom; Yves was attempting to read, while Darren stowed his hold-all.

On the bridge Grant listened to the storm sounds - a yowling blast, rattling rain, the slapping thud of hundreds of tons of salt water which scaled the ship's side like a marauding pirate crew. The wind had touched 60 m.p.h., and the barometric pressure was still plunging. Grant couldn't delay a moment longer. 'Call the ol' man on the intercom.'

'No need.' Alexander stood there beside him. The first officer felt a surge of relief. James Alexander was back in charge. Grant briefed him.

Under beetling brows the captain's eyes flitted across panels and dials. Grant had followed proper procedures: reducing engine speed to seven knots and steering *Sea Shepherd* into wind and waves. 'Good work, Phil. This one's gonna be *real* hell...'

Dimly visible at dawn were thirty-foot waves, crowned by as much again in seething spray. Military-looking low clouds closed in, rank by rank, lancing rain on everything beneath. Soon the wind screamed past the 75 m.p.h. mark. Force 12. That made it official: a hurricane.

Alexander cursed himself. Fool! Why hadn't he interpreted the signs - lurid sunset, slick dark sea? A double-page advertisement for a hurricane! Up-to-the-minute weather forecasts must have alerted him, even before the radio was knocked out. Had he received but failed to heed them? Whatever the truth, *he* was responsible, *he* was to blame. If his ship foundered...

He could only guess at the diameter of the hurricane - 50 miles, 100, 1,000 - and at its direction. Nor could he know how close *Sea Shepherd* was to the storm centre, a vortex where the all-powerful wind shrilled and shouted like a multitude of fiends.

By now Vanessa and Susan were taking turns at the sink. Next door, Yves and Darren collided involuntarily and gave up pretending to ignore each other. In the neighbouring cabin Gary ushered queasy Norman to the bottom bunk, then ventured into the corridor.

Cannoning off the metal bulkheads, he zigzagged a few bruising yards, determined to find someone - anyone - who could give him news. From every quarter came the unnerving noise of objects in the process of destruction.

Ben Bellingham tottered into sight. Maude Mimpriss, limp and ghastly white, hung on his arm. 'Back to your cabin, young man!' Ben's gruffness didn't encourage discussion.

Captain Alexander felt old, too old for this. Hour after hour. The bridge floor had become an unyielding trampoline. Often *Sea Shepherd* was hidden. A rehearsal for the time when the wild water claimed her completely? He crumpled the thought like a ball of paper. The officer who'd relieved Grant on watch chanted statistics in the captain's ear. Wind speed: 120 m.p.h. Wave-height: 40 feet. Barometer reading: 903 millibars, down to a record low.

Johnny Masterson arrived on the bridge, bringing what information he could. 'Curtis has had no luck with the radio...Baggalley and Stokes are supervising the teenagers.'

Below and aft of them, the Chief Engineer nursed the engines, wincing whenever the ship's propellers were forced from the sea to thresh in deafening impotence.

Amidships, Senior Laboratory Scientist Frederick Cairns confronted different problems. His prized fish specimens, slopping against the tank walls, were suffering torment. Some, incredibly, were being seasick. He'd attend to them later. Such was his preoccupation that it never occurred to him there might not *be* a later.

Alexander muttered, unable to see ahead. But when the curtains of spray parted, he wished they hadn't. Combers, peaking at fifty feet, were queuing up to board *Sea Shepherd*.

At 1.00 p.m. precisely, a hurricane squall topped 150 m.p.h. Could things get any worse? With a crack like a gunshot the bridge window shattered. Glass fragments flew, slashing flesh. The helmsman's gurgling shriek was swamped by a thousand-times-louder outcry as the wet wind ran amok. It set out to strip him, ballooning clothes, ripping seams. He staggered backwards, his face a horrific network of red rivulets.

Alexander fought to keep a clear head. Two priorities: look

after that poor devil and regain control of the wheel. The wheel was the more urgent. Charts, papers spiralled in a bizarre blizzard. 'Move, damn you!' The men with him seemed temporarily stupefied. Exerting every muscle against a solid stream of air, he led them across the treacherously pitching floor.

'She's broaching!' Alexander bellowed. All somehow found extra strength, well aware of the consequences if the waves caught *Sea Shepherd* broadside. Men grabbed the wheel, risking broken fingers. But the ship was too far gone, heeling more and more acutely to starboard as the heaped water leaned on her. Nobody remained standing.

The inclinometer, a device measuring the angle of roll, indicated 38 degrees...39...40. No vessel could recover from a 45-degree list in weather conditions like these. James Alexander, defeated and belittled by self-loathing, prepared for the end. He was losing his ship. And he'd betrayed the trust of crew and passengers, who would pay with their lives.

The captain did not believe in God. But as the inclinometer edged towards 44 degrees, something was about to change his mind. At two hundred miles an hour a caterwauling gust slammed into the port side of the ship, shouldering her on to an even keel. Agile and adroit, Alexander recaptured the helm. He governed the engines, coaxing *Sea Shepherd* - slowly, sluggishly - to obey. She was coming round! Ready and able to brave the storm's full onslaught.

Later Alexander would say his first prayer of thanks for forty years. Now he must act. While a rating tended the injured man, Alexander put out a call for the medical officer.

The below-decks scene suggested a visit by rampaging vandals. Buckled equipment, up-ended furniture, spattered provisions. Throughout the length and breadth of the vessel, people assessed the damage. To themselves included.

The thrust of providence that had saved *Sea Shepherd* also heralded a further twist in the hurricane's behaviour. Instead of charging head-on, the wind now withdrew for seconds at a time - to return on irregular raids. From all points of the compass. Drilling

100

tunnels in the spume-laden atmosphere, it hit the ship like dynamite explosions.

Philip Grant, who had resumed bridge duties, was perplexed; Alexander less so. If his theory proved correct, those aboard were due for perhaps the eeriest experience on earth. He'd been told about the eye of the hurricane - an arena of supernatural stillness at the storm's dead centre. Were the accounts accurate?

Conjecture gave way to stunned disbelief as *Sea Shepherd* bore them into a slow motion dream. A spotlight sun shone on waters that were polished ebony yet transparent. The air, warm and soggy and stationary, made skins prickle with perspiration. And the hush... awesomely 'loud'. But beyond the borders of this bewitched haven - a fifteen-mile circle - the hurricane howled more malevolently than ever.

No longer cooped up, Gary and Susan embraced in the corridor. He wasn't surprised by her greenish complexion or the tale of woe that went with it. Yves and Vanessa, though less demonstrative, were clearly pleased to see each other. Darren and Norman stretched legs, stiff from lack of exercise.

Meanwhile, traipsing through debris, officers and maintenance personnel conducted a systematic inspection. The engine-room had escaped almost unscathed. Equally heartening, *Sea Shepherd*'s hull was keeping the Caribbean where it belonged - outside. And what of the casualties? Astonishingly minor. Grazes, sprains, bumps. Apart from the helmsman, strapped down in the ship's hospital, no one was seriously hurt.

Ben Bellingham informed passengers that the rock'n'roll marathon would continue. 'This is just an intermission, I'm afraid. Make the most of it.'

As Gary rearranged their cabin, Norman felt fit enough to impart another portion of his knowledge. 'A hurricane may discharge $1\frac{1}{2}$ billion gallons of rain, you know. Once, in the Philippines, 42 inches fell in 24 hours.' Gary stopped what he was doing. Hands on hips, he stared at Norman and laughed. Some things never change.

Not a hint of humour brightened the captain's countenance.

Alexander, sticky and panting in the humidity, stepped aside to let ship's carpenters block the holed window with planks. A wind-blown bolt was the missile that had caused the calamity. Morosely he took stock. Everything on the dented deck was bent or broken. Four of the eight lifeboats had gone.

'Radio's operating, Captain.' A haggard Leslie Curtis. 'We picked up Miami - US Weather Bureau. The hurricane's heading north-west. They've dubbed it Hannah. It's Category 5, severe...'

'Severe, eh?' Alexander's mouth curved sarcastically. 'I rather gathered that.'

Curtis passed on the rest of the relevant data. If he expected congratulations, he was disappointed.

Hannah - so the bitch had a name. Alexander half suspected she had a mind too, a scheming mind. This notion seemed more probable when the hurricane renewed her assault and, amid mountainous waves, *Sea Shepherd* cast off a propeller.

Yet again the youngsters were toppled. They sat or lay now among their scattered possessions. At once Darren began to scoop up the spilt contents of his hold-all. Yves gawped, seized by sudden indignation. He lunged at Darren. 'Hey, that's my pen!' 'Is it?' 'Yes, it is. Where'd you get it?' 'Found it.' 'Where?' 'C-c-can't remember.' Retrieving the pen, Yves stomped out of the cabin.

Above deck, Alexander argued heatedly with the Chief Engineer via the telephone that connected bridge and engine-room. The engineer hadn't minced his words: on only one propeller and at four knots, *Sea Shepherd* was going nowhere - except to the bottom. Philip Grant, a fine officer whose courage could stretch no further, shared these fears and said so. Alexander faced him. Glaring, he bit back a scornful retort. 'Come on, Phil, we weren't spared for nothing. After fifteen hours I flatly refuse to become shark food.'

Was the captain's faith genuine, or faked? Somehow his ship, twice as difficult to steer, clung for dear life to the switchbacking ocean. Hannah harried them until her very last gasp.

And then, quite suddenly, *Sea Shepherd* was tossing in water that was merely rough. From a rent in the clouds gold rays fanned across the sky and gilded the billows. It was over!

The captain retired to his cabin, where Ben Bellingham found him, hands clasped and apparently talking to himself. Ben crept away.

On deck that night, Susan said to Gary: 'No wonder he's called Alexander the Great.'

9 Revelations

It took a lot to annoy Yves, who would rather forgive and forget than let resentment fester. Despite everything, he'd been willing to tolerate his unco-operative room-mate. But that was before Darren stole the pen. A thief, there could be no doubt.

'Why didn't I punch him on the nose?' Yves was still fuming as he passed Vanessa and Susan's door. Shall I tell them about Darren? He kept moving. Tell one of the teachers, Ben or the captain? He couldn't think straight.

Five minutes later he was back in the cabin. Darren had retreated beneath a bunk blanket. Yves said nothing, biding his time.

The time to speak out came next day. After breakfast, ingeniously prepared in the post-hurricane galley, Darren rose and left the others. Now, having considered carefully, Yves produced his pen. Vanessa reached for it. 'Where...?'

'Darren's bag. He said he found it.'

Susan kicked Gary under the table.

'Maybe he did find it,' Vanessa offered weakly.

'Yeah, in my drawer!'

Norman toyed with a spoon. 'What are you going to do, Yves?'

'Search through his belongings, that's what. And I want you all to be there.'

Vanessa protested: 'We *can't*. It's not right.'

But Yves' mind was made up. 'Suit yourselves. I'll just have to handle this alone.' Taking the pen from Vanessa, he stalked out of the dining-room. As he expected, four figures followed him.

Darren was absent from the cabin. While Norman stood guard outside, Yves emptied the hold-all on to the bottom bunk. Vanessa exclaimed, identifying her watch. There was more 'loot': a pocket calculator, a lighter, officers' brass buttons, ship's cutlery, a bundle of ten-dollar bills, a sealed packet, an orange pennant bearing the words FRIENDS OF THE SEA OTTER. Seeing this last item, Susan had to giggle. 'How on earth...?'

Three sharp raps at the door. Norman. Soon after, the door swung open - and in walked Darren. He froze. Only his eyes moved, missing no detail. Then, defiantly, he advanced to the bunk. 'Hands off! That stuff's private, personal. I'll...'

'Report us?' Yves jeered. 'Go ahead. You can explain how Vanessa's watch jumped into your bag.'

Darren wheeled, as if to break away, but the escape route was barred by Gary and Norman.

'Sit down!' An authoritative Yves.

A deflated Darren sat beside the objects laid out like exhibits in a courtroom. The trial was due to commence.

Yves picked up the first 'exhibit' - knives and forks inscribed with *Sea Shepherd*'s name. 'You stole these, didn't you?' He tossed them back on to the bunk. 'And the buttons. And this.' He waved the pennant.

Susan interrupted: 'Why, Darren? I thought you liked Rhonda.'

Any possibility of a reply was curtailed by Yves, determined to complete his case. One by one he held the confiscated possessions under Darren's nose. The calculator - whose?

'Hey, I bet it belongs to Peter Stokes,' Vanessa piped up, remembering that the maths master had 'mislaid' his.

The lighter. Yves continued remorselessly. Next he riffled the wad of notes. 'Rob a bank?'

Finally Yves came to the brown-paper packet. He kneaded with inquiring fingers, then passed it round to the others. 'What's inside, I wonder? Something secret. Give it here, Gary.'

He started to tear the paper.

'No!' The anguished yell shook Yves rigid. Darren was trembling. 'Please... Don't...'

The semicircle of accusers changed conspicuously. Nobody wanted this - Darren in tears. Susan wished she were somewhere else.

Gary, who'd begun to think Yves was relishing the role of prosecutor, intervened: 'OK. Enough's enough. Darren, we'll wait outside and leave you in peace for a bit. But we'll be back for some answers.'

Whether or not whole-heartedly, Yves accompanied them. Gary expressed concern that they all keep their heads. 'He's entitled to a fair hearing.' Norman nodded.

After a short interval the five re-entered the cabin. Darren was dry eyed, on his feet. An air of challenge hung about him, like a boxer ready to counter-punch. Gary took over. 'Well, what've you got to say for yourself?'

Darren glowered, his mouth a thin hard line.

'Not talking, eh?' Gary said mildly. 'I can understand that, in a way. You'd probably prefer to answer to someone else - Ben Bellingham, for example.'

Darren jerked forward a pace, driven to respond. 'Drop dead, busybody! You're bluffing. Can't prove a thing.'

'Oh no?' Gary side-stepped him and snatched up the orange pennant.

'Rhonda *gave* it to me,' Darren retorted.

'That's a lie,' Susan declared. 'Rhonda told Vanessa and me they didn't have a spare flag.'

While this was going on, Norman examined the lighter. 'L.C.' he uttered. 'What do those initials stand for? L.C.' Without wanting to, he'd become the focus of attention. 'I know...Leslie Curtis! He's a smoker.'

Darren's denial was emphatic. 'Rubbish! Just a coincidence.'

Gary shrugged, seeming not to care. 'It's easy enough to check. We'll ask him.'

Suddenly Darren lost his cockiness, the boxer's nerve had gone.

Sensing victory, Yves returned to the attack. Before Gary could stop him, he was undoing the packet. Darren surrendered at once, pleading with his hands. Yves relented. The torn paper revealed a flat, black - book cover? 'What is it, Darren? And why are you so scared?'

'I don't know. Really...honestly...I promise. It's Curtis's. I'm to look after it. If anything happens to him, I've got to give it to the captain.'

Sceptical, contemptuous, Yves widened the hole in the paper. 'Expect us to believe that? Who'd trust *you*?'

'It's the truth! Please don't open it. Curtis will...My dad...' Darren was reduced to incoherence.

Gary regained control of the situation. 'OK, OK, nobody's gonna lynch you. But you must come clean, tell us everything.'

Drawing a deep breath, Darren recounted his story - falteringly at first and then with a kind of feverish fluency. The revelations could hardly have been more startling.

He recalled *Sea Shepherd*'s departure from Southampton, seven months ago, when he'd joined the fortunate few on a voyage of discovery that his schoolmates envied. It should have been the best day of his life. Instead it was one of the worst. Thanks to Curtis!

Soon after boarding, Darren was singled out by the radio officer, whose apparent kindness proved false. And then the blackmail began.

'Curtis knew all about me - and my family. Said he'd make trouble, big trouble, if I didn't do exactly as I was told. He knew that I, well, I...take things. Can't help it. It's like an illness.'

'Kleptomania,' Norman supplied.

Vanessa: 'Klepto-what?'

'Kleptomania. A compulsive urge to steal.'

'That's the word,' Darren confirmed. 'That's what the doctor called it.'

He resumed his narrative, which grew stranger by the minute. His father was serving a prison sentence for theft - and would not come out alive, Curtis had sworn, unless Darren 'obeyed'. The boy gestured helplessly. 'He means it. I daren't cross him.'

Outraged, Susan interjected: 'The swine! I never liked him. But I don't understand what use you are to him.'

Darren lowered his head guiltily. 'I, er, spy and eavesdrop on people. Anybody, everybody. And whatever I find out, I pass on to Curtis. He says I can go places he couldn't without causing suspicion.'

Yves' budding sympathy withered at this confession. 'A nasty little tell-tale, aren't you?'

Darren didn't try to excuse himself but proceeded with the story. Guarding the packet was his most important job, he said, and *no one* must learn of the contents - except in an emergency. Curtis had paid him, in dollar bills. Darren owned up to further 'crimes', even to the fire he hadn't meant to start.

His painful explanation over, he awaited their verdict in a lengthening silence. Yves broke it. 'We'll have to see Ben or the captain right away. There's no choice.'

Darren's face contorted. 'But...'

Gary cut across him. 'Hang on, Yves. If his father's in danger... Curtis can't be operating alone and could have heavies to do his dirty work. This needs thinking about.'

'What's behind it all?' Susan was bewildered.

'Your guess is as good as mine,' said Gary. 'But Curtis and Co. are no supporters of The Eden Mission.'

The debate ebbed and flowed until they reached a provisional agreement. They'd leave Stokes's calculator on his desk at the next opportunity, and find a way of replacing other stolen items.

'As for Curtis,' added Gary, 'we'll watch his every move. *You*, Darren, will be *our* undercover man.' He jabbed a finger. 'And remember, you're on probation. No more thieving - or else!'

Two thousand miles to the west, in his Houston office, Art Benton sat stiffly. 'Call from Zurich, Switzerland,' his secretary announced. Benton felt his stomach tighten. Zurich, home of...

The Director.

Benton listened to the unmistakable tones - soft, lisping, mid-European - of a man he had never seen, whose name he did not know, immensely powerful and influential.

'That fiasco off Santa Barbara!' The Director simmered. 'Who authorised the ramming of the ecologists' boat? You?'

'I'm not that dumb.'

'Who, then? It was clumsy, rash and pointless.'

Benton answered slowly: 'I've a hunch, no more.'

'Yes!'

'My money's on Max Kruger.'

'Kruger, hmmm,' The Director mused. 'Possible. An over-ambitious hothead who employs crude methods and cruder operatives. Quite possible.'

'So what shall I do?' queried Benton.

'Do? Absolutely nothing. Leave Kruger to me.'

The line went dead. Benton hung up. He dried his damp palms on a handkerchief.

Seconds later, in Zurich, The Director's phone rang. Maximilian Kruger calling.

Though the hurricane had long abated, every hour brought fresh evidence of Hannah's handiwork. Captain Alexander felt downright pity for *Sea Shepherd*, mauled, maimed and sorely in need of rest and recuperation. He and his company were busier now than at the height of the storm. Mopping up and running repairs disrupted normal schedules. Other matters, such as finding the saboteur, must wait.

On deck, two ratings cleaned out the swimming-pool - in which the corpse of a large sea-bird appeared to be browsing among assorted junk.

Below, lab scientist Frederick Cairns talked to and fed his surviving fish.

In the ship's hospital an orderly tended the helmsman, whose

109

stitched face would heal and whose eyes, by God's grace, had not been punctured.

It was a starry night with a lemon-slice moon when *Sea Shepherd* finally found a berth - and a deserved respite - at Port of Spain, Trinidad. Crowding the rail, the teenagers gazed across the multicoloured scribble of harbour lights on the water to the inviting island beyond. While the ship underwent a three-week refit, including a period in dry dock to attach a new propeller, they vowed to take full advantage of this unplanned pause in the voyage.

The days dissolved into each other. For a few of the crew there was the luxury of a little shore leave. For most, however, the stay meant work and more work.

Varied messages poured in through the radio and satellite receivers. Ben Bellingham was delighted to hear that the otters had eluded the oil's slimy embrace and that some were being relocated in less hazardous areas.

But this was his sole cause for rejoicing.

Next he learned about the mini-submarine, still missing. Not so the two men with it. Their mutilated bodies, washed up on a beach, lay in a California morgue. Soon after, another bombshell - a radio call from the abducted trawler skipper, freed so he could deliver a short speech from his captor: 'We'll meet again, Bellingham. And then you die.'

During these weeks Leslie Curtis gained the distinct and disquieting impression of being shadowed. Also that someone had been snooping in his cabin. He was right on both counts.

Ashore, Susan and Gary sampled the pleasures of sugar-cane and calypso music. But, unable to forget recent events, the pair made apathetic tourists.

Returning to ship, Gary looked up at the cloudless sky. A red seaplane was circling the harbour.

10 Jungle

Darren padded along a ship's corridor. Since 'owning up', he didn't feel quite so alone, so oppressed. Maybe things *would* turn out all right...

'Urrrgh!' He was wrenched violently sideways. A hard and heavy hand transferred itself from his collar to the scruff of his neck. Curtis slammed the store-room door behind them and released his grip. Darren spun around. Curtis had never looked more menacing.

'I wanna word with you, sonny. Been shooting your mouth off, haven't you?'

'No.' Darren stepped back. 'I dunno what you're on about.'

Curtis closed in. 'Yes you do. Blabbing our business to those other brats.'

The boy's heart missed a beat. 'No, I couldn't. You *know* I couldn't - even if I wanted to.'

With slit eyes the radio officer weighed him up. Each second seemed a minute.

Eventually Curtis spoke: 'Then why've they been following me? Sniggering, whispering. There's always one of 'em around.'

Darren wrinkled his forehead, as if pondering the puzzle. 'I've no idea,' he lied again. 'It's not my fault none of my friends like you.'

'Friends!' Curtis guffawed. 'You haven't got any friends.'

'Well, they like me better than you.' Now Darren was telling the truth.

111

Curtis's rage fizzled out into irritable uncertainty. He began to pace, wondering aloud. Who'd searched his quarters? Darren was unable to help here either. Next Curtis complained: 'Ever since the fire, the captain's had it in for me.'

Darren displayed fresh interest. 'How *did* the blaze start? Are you sure you didn't leave a cigarette burning?'

'That s'posed to be funny?' snarled Curtis. 'Don't get lippy with me, kid.'

'Sorry.' Darren adopted a conciliatory expression. 'I just thought...you've, um, had a lot on your mind.' Slyly he added: 'And perhaps you're imagining things - about the others, I mean.'

Curtis conveyed his contempt, but confusion was detectable too. 'OK, that'll do for now.' Darren turned to the door.

A parting demand from Curtis: 'Bring the packet. Tomorrow, 8.30 a.m. sharp.'

After lessons and a rushed lunch, Susan, Gary, Vanessa, Yves and Norman headed across the deck to an out-of-the-way corner by the stern. Darren was already there.

'*Well?*' Curiosity and eagerness mingled in Susan's voice.

Darren divulged the details of his unceremonious encounter with Curtis. Despite himself, Yves felt a sneaking admiration.

'So he's asked for the packet?' Gary checked.

Darren nodded. 'He *borrows* it from time to time, don't know why. When I get it back it's been newly wrapped and sealed.'

Vanessa: 'Good thing Yves didn't tear the paper to shreds. But how will you explain the hole?'

'I'll think of something... Storm damage?' A hint of humour, the first they'd ever discerned in Darren.

'Of course!' Norman took off his glasses. 'What fools we've been!'

The rest of them were accustomed to occasional outbursts from their 'eccentric professor'.

'The sabotage,' Norman babbled on. 'Don't you see? Curtis - he's the perpetrator.'

Gary's jaw dropped. 'Old Norman's right. Curtis could be the one, prob'ly is. Why didn't it dawn on us before?'

'I vote we go to the captain,' said Yves.

'Not yet,' Gary cautioned, 'not without evidence.'

Norman again: 'Bet there's evidence in the packet - in the book.'

'Maybe,' conceded Gary. 'But we've got Darren to think of. Besides, from what he's told us, Curtis is clearly getting rattled. Let's pile on the pressure.'

An animated conference ensued, hatching several schemes to make life intolerable for the radio officer.

As the group dispersed, Susan put her arm round a suddenly crestfallen Darren. She guessed the reason. 'Don't worry, we won't let anything happen to your dad.'

Sea Shepherd - four hours out from Port of Spain and four days away from the Amazon - should be bravely buoyant, not trailing her troubles like wake. James Alexander loved his ship as if she breathed, thought, felt. Sometimes he fancied they were partners who 'understood' each other. This was such a moment. In his cabin, flanked by Bellingham and Masterson, Alexander tried to sound positive. Quite a challenge, given the facts. Fact One: the deceased submariners, both good men. Letters of condolence to their relatives had been sincere but inadequate. Fact Two: the death threat to Ben. Fact Three: the saboteur. Still at large. Still free to plot and execute another, perhaps a more destructive, strike. Exasperated, Alexander rounded unfairly on Johnny Masterson: 'Some security officer!'

Early next morning Darren approached the radio room with trepidation. Casually confident when he'd answered Vanessa, he was by no means certain of conning Curtis about the torn paper. He must be utterly convincing.

Here goes! Darren tapped on the radio room door. It opened at once. Curtis bundled him inside. 'Let's have it.' Darren unbuttoned his shirt and pulled out the packet.

'What's this?' Curtis's reaction was predictable. 'I warned you!'

Fortunately for Darren the radio receiver intervened. While Curtis was taking down the message, Darren deftly pocketed a couple of cigarettes from the pack on the table beside him.

Curtis signed off. 'Right...'

Darren's chance. 'The hurricane, it made a pigsty of our cabin. Everything was flying around, including my hold-all. I'm surprised the paper isn't more badly ripped.'

So plausible and unrepentant was the boy that his inquisitor soon seemed satisfied. He dismissed Darren, but only after a pointed reference to his father.

The remark would have a profound effect, the opposite of what was intended. Something inside Darren had snapped. An icy resolve crystallised in his mind, colder by far than any fear. For his own sake, for the sake of his mum, for the sake of his dad, he'd 'fix' Curtis.

Darren became the keenest member of the youngsters' team, playing a cat-and-mouse game with Curtis. Three days' sailing lay between them and the Amazon. You could do a lot in three days.

Throughout lessons that morning, Darren made a poor pupil. But he was wholly attentive when maths master Peter Stokes stood up, looking ridiculously pleased, and addressed the class. 'I've found my calculator! Darndest thing is, I searched for ages and it was buried under these files.' Of all Darren's mixed and complicated emotions, happy relief predominated.

In the afternoons the youngsters often went their separate ways, pursuing individual interests. But today they shared a common purpose: to bait and bamboozle the radio officer. And they wouldn't relent. Not today, not tomorrow, not the day after.

Darren and Norman were of similar build with brownish hair. From behind, each could be mistaken for the other. Darren owned a lurid-green, white-striped anorak - a familiar sight around the ship and an eyesore to somebody who had Vanessa's dress sense. This garish garment added brilliance to the team tactics. First Darren wore it, then Norman, as they presented their backs to Curtis, disappearing round corners and reappearing tantalisingly out of range. At one stage the radio officer hailed Darren in a corridor and 'gave chase', only to unhand a politely forgiving Norman.

Before long Curtis glimpsed the anorak again. Darren briefly showed his face. Later, sporting a cap to conceal his darker hair, Gary joined in the charade.

By evening Curtis's nerves were ticking under a skin that felt too tight. Knocks at the door, and nobody there...his name called repeatedly...Darren, everywhere. A rational man, Curtis didn't doubt his own logic. The brats, they were fooling around. He decided to ignore them and their adolescent pranks.

But as he retired for the night, he noticed - on the bunk-side table - a cigarette-stub and burn mark. Did I...? No. And his shaving kit, always methodically stowed above the wash-basin, now sat on a chair. What the hell's going on?

Darren might have enjoyed sweet dreams had he known that the radio officer was tossing and turning through a nightmare peopled by figures in green anoraks.

Next day dawned bright and innocent and full of promise - another golden opportunity to torment Curtis!

Whispering over breakfast, within earshot of the adults, Gary let his voice rise: 'I wouldn't want to be in his black book.' Curtis flinched, as though pricked by a pin. He quickly regained his composure. Several minutes later, with elaborate unconcern, he got up and left the dining-room.

It was afternoon before they were able to resume their game of psychology. Again Gary led the team into action. By telling a joke - 'A magician and his parrot are adrift on a raft after their ship sinks. Eventually the sulky parrot squawks: "OK, I give up. WHAT'VE YOU DONE WITH THE SHIP?"' The punch line, followed by forced laughter, was timed to coincide with Curtis's arrival on deck. He scowled. A saboteur's scowl?

Never tiring, never growing bored, the six kept on 'playing'.

At dusk, after dinner, Vanessa deliberately walked into Curtis outside his cabin. Her smile was particularly beguiling and held him long enough for her to indulge in some girlish chatter. His hostile stare softened. Vanessa's charm, like her perfume, was strong stuff.

Bending forward confidentially, she said it was a shame he was unpopular with the other officers. Curtis bristled. 'What?' Vanessa's hand flew to her mouth. 'Oh...forgive me. I shouldn't have spoken.' She peered past him, ill at ease and reluctant to say more; or apparently so. But Curtis insisted. Sighing, Vanessa was persuaded to disclose: 'I heard Captain Alexander and First Officer Grant talking about you. Called you,' she hesitated, 'incompetent. I didn't catch everything, but I think they mentioned putting one of your deputies in charge of the radio room.'

Curtis's face was a picture. Vanessa's, too, though artfully contrived. 'Never mind,' she uttered. 'They probably don't mean it.'

Only one day off, the Amazon began to exert a magnetic pull on crew and passengers alike. Thoughts and talk were already being borne along the river's broad waters, which would carry *Sea Shepherd* deep into the jungle. But the teenagers had not finished with Curtis yet. Sufficient time remained to give him an extra sharp prod before the ship docked at Belem in Brazil.

This was masterminded by Darren and Norman. Its success depended on the unwitting co-operation of Curtis. Would he wear his uniform jacket to the meal table?

Yes, he obliged.

During the meal suspense mounted. Coffee came. Now, Curtis fumbled for a cigarette, asking the Chief Engineer for a light and grumbling yet again about his lost lighter. The youngsters watched.

Curtis was jittery and obviously too warm. Perspiration beaded his brow. He tugged at the white handkerchief in his breast-pocket... and out fell, clattering on to the table, his initialled lighter.

There was a lull in proceedings at that moment. Nobody missed the incident - or the sight of a totally baffled radio officer. 'The man's cracking up.' An audible comment from Grant.

Afterwards Susan caught herself feeling sorry for Curtis and more than a little guilty. 'Are we being fair?'

'*Fair?*' Gary was incredulous. 'Has *he* been fair? To Darren, to his father, to us, to Captain Alexander, to Ben, to The Eden...?'

'Do leave off, Gary! I only asked.'

116

He apologised, adding: 'Anyway, let's forget Curtis for now.'

Belem beckoned, the Amazon's Atlantic port. Beyond, through the infinite emerald forest, flowed a river wider than the English Channel, deep enough for an ocean-going vessel to sail 2,300 miles inland, so long that it traverses almost all of South America.

On deck, in a balmy breeze, the students strained their senses - as if to pick up the first scent and song of the jungle. Ben Bellingham ambled over, joining in. 'It's a bit early yet. We're still miles off-shore.'

With Ben's permission Norman fetched a bucket and rope to conduct an experiment. He lowered the bucket into the sea, hauled it up and invited his friends to dip their fingers. 'Taste.'

'Nothing special.' Vanessa's verdict. 'It's like tap-water.'

Norman beamed triumphantly. 'But we're at sea! Should be salty.'

Vanessa tut-tutted. 'I fell for that one, didn't I?'

'I did too,' Susan admitted under her breath. Then, speaking up, she inquired: 'How do you account for the phenomenon, Professor?'

Norman was ready to enlighten them. 'Well, because it's discharged with such force from the Amazon's mouth, fresh water extends for a hundred miles.'

Ben departed, chuckling. 'Quite a river, eh?'

The Brazilian coast, once a sketched suggestion, was taking on colour and contours. *Sea Shepherd* beelined for Belem. 'Soon be there,' Gary told Susan, trying to sound casual. But the ship crawled to a halt and dropped anchor some distance from the port.

Susan groaned comically. What now? A boat zipped towards them - the start of a tedious round of formalities. Customs declarations, health clearance, checking and re-checking immigration papers. Although Alexander knew he could short cut the process by giving the Customs men 'presents' of whisky and cigarettes, he stubbornly refused. The questions, in passable English, kept coming. Occasionally Grant introduced a Portuguese phrase in an attempt to disarm the inspectors. They remained stony faced.

After two hours, and considerable haggling, *Sea Shepherd* was

117

allowed to berth.

While the ship loaded fuel and stores, a party went ashore - Ben Bellingham to consult a leading Amazon environmentalist, teenagers and tutors as sightseers.

Late that night Susan lay staring into the dark. *I've just got to talk.* She found the cabin carpet with her bare feet and stood up. 'Vanessa?' The softly snoring form didn't budge.

'Vanessa!'

'Uhhh...'

Susan shook her gently. 'You awake?'

'I am *now*.' Her petulance was understandable. 'Whatever's the matter?'

'I can't sleep.'

'So you decided to wake me!'

'I'm really sorry, Vanessa, but I keep thinking about what we saw today in the market. Those dolphins' eyes, used for brooches and voodoo rites...the poor little monkeys in cages...and the spotted animal skin that horrible man was selling secretly behind his stall...'

'I know what you mean. Sickening - and spooky.' Vanessa reached out and touched her. 'Still, the day wasn't all bad. I enjoyed walking round the church, even Mimpriss's commentary. And the market full of medicinal herbs from the forest was interesting too. Don't dwell on the unpleasant things.' She yawned. 'Now *I'm* going back to sleep.'

Susan withdrew. 'Yes...thanks.' Suddenly she felt very drowsy.

There were two new faces at breakfast - pilots who, taking turns on the bridge for four days and nights, would guide *Sea Shepherd* a thousand miles up river to a heart-of-the-jungle city with 1¼ million inhabitants. Manaus.

Goodbye Belem, and good riddance! Susan, leaning against Gary, watched *Sea Shepherd* untied and set free.

Some hours later the ship swung to starboard - entering the aptly named Narrows. No more than a hundred yards or so wide. Bordered by jungle. Vanessa, Norman, Yves and Darren darted to and fro across the deck. Gary could almost believe *Sea Shepherd*

118

was parting the trees with her bow. Susan studied the green wall of forest, longing to see beyond, be beyond; in a creation tumultuous and alien...

Darren brought her back with a bump. 'Look!' Along the bank, huts on stilts. Children, copper-skinned and laughing, launched their dug-out canoes.

'*Caboclos* - the water people,' Darren said, surprising Susan. 'Descendants of mixed marriages between the Portuguese settlers and Amazon Indians. They live by fishing.'

Joyful hoots as the canoes cavorted in *Sea Shepherd*'s wash.

Philip Grant and Johnny Masterson appeared, carrying customary plastic bags of gifts. These were lobbed astern to the *Caboclos* children.

Regretfully Susan left her chosen post on the starboard rail. Arm in arm with Gary, she made for Bellingham's lecture.

A row of canvas chairs had been set out near the stern, Susan and Gary took the last empty places. The teachers sat with Ben at a table. 'Right,' he said. 'Now we're all here, I'll begin. Or rather, Mr. Baggalley will. He's going to tell you a bit about the Amazon's geography and history.'

Geoffrey Baggalley rose. Yves slumped in his chair, resigned to a dull discourse. But, like the others, he was soon listening to every word.

'*Nothing* about the Amazon is average,' Baggalley asserted. 'It deserves a record book all to itself. The Equator runs through the river's mouth - 200 miles from side to side - which also accommodates an island the size of Switzerland. A long way inland, the banks are still forty miles apart. Water-levels vary by an astounding 45 feet, depending on the season. And although we've arrived during the dry season, you'll be glad you packed your plastic raincoats.'

He paused, mopping his forehead in the muggy heat. 'I won't stifle you with statistics. The Amazon is born as a humble brook high in the snow-capped Andes, only 120 miles from the Pacific, and steadily swells for 4,000 miles to push back the Atlantic.

119

Seventeen of its tributaries are greater than the Rhine...'

A clink of glasses as iced lemonade was distributed by a steward, thanks to thoughtful Philip Grant.

With refreshed energy the speaker proceeded. 'So much for this remarkable river. But even that is put in the shade, if you'll pardon the pun, by the Amazon rain forest. It's the world's largest, spreading 2½ million square miles across two-fifths of South America and into eight countries. Brazil claims most of it; Bolivia, Peru, Colombia, Venezuela, Surinam, Guyana and Ecuador share the rest.'

He helped himself to more lemonade from a jug.

'As you know, rain forests play a key role in regulating regional and global climate. And they're *very* old. Europe's forests, for instance, have existed a mere 11,000 years - one ten-thousandth of the Amazon's age!' Baggalley scratched his head. 'I promised to go easy on statistics, didn't I?'

However, nobody in the audience felt hard done by. Gary wished all lessons could be like this. Utterly absorbed he let the teacher take him back hundreds of millions of years...when the Amazon was part of Gondwanaland, a super-continent including South America, Africa, India, Australia and Antarctica. Then, flying through time, Gary alighted in the 'recent past' - just 10,000 years ago - trekking south with the Indians, over land that spanned the Bering Straits, to colonise their present jungle home. 'There are 250 known tribes, but maybe more will be discovered. For the Indians' sake I rather hope not.'

Susan: 'Will you tell us the story of how the Amazon got its name?'

Starchy Maude Mimpriss registered disapproval at the interruption, but Baggalley always welcomed a spontaneous question.

So he began the tale of Spanish captain Francisco de Orellana, the first European to travel the river's full length. In 1541 Orellana and sixty men set out from the west. Soon they were suffering starvation. They raided native villages for provisions. On one such foray they were confronted by warriors armed with bows and arrows, and a battle ensued. These frightening foes were...female. Later described as *white* and tall and very robust, they reminded Orellana of the warrior women of Greek mythology.

'The Amazons!' Norman exclaimed.'

'Exactly,' said Baggalley.'

Concluding his talk, the teacher handed over to Ben. But almost immediately, the ship's loud-speakers boomed out. MR. BELLINGHAM TO THE DATA-CONTROL CENTRE, PLEASE...MR. BELLINGHAM TO DATA-CONTROL...

Frowning, he expressed his regrets and strode off. Susan and Gary rose, stretched and sauntered to the rail. The tawny water rolled by between them and the jungle. They returned to their seats as a rating brought word from Ben - the lecture was postponed.

Disappointed but pleased to be at liberty, the students chatted for a while and then divided into pairs. Norman, however, scurried away to write up his notes. Darren disappeared too. In the cabin he undid his hold-all and removed a freshly wrapped packet, fondling it as though it were a precious possession. Perhaps it was. Perhaps it was worth Curtis's neck.

Daylight dimmed; darkness would descend abruptly. Before that, though, a brief and vivid interlude. Trees silhouetted against a marmalade sky...a pink dolphin somersaulting to say hello...the spine-tingling start of a symphony of night noises.

Peter Stokes nearly flattened Vanessa in the dash to fetch his camera. 'And they tell *us* to mind our manners,' she remarked to Yves with mock indignation. Yves moved closer, enjoying her company at least as much as the tropical vista.

Minute by minute the symphony gained volume and variety. Trills, cackles... What a hullabaloo! Susan thought. Like nothing she'd ever heard. But one discord dominated, made her shiver: a penetrating chorus pouring from the forest, up to the sunset and across its mirrored embers. Howler monkeys. Their voices carried three miles, more mournful than wolves, more unearthly than a flight of phantoms. Putting a curse on trespassers? Susan's reference book, although comprehensive, hadn't prepared her for *this*. She could well believe that men lost in the green gloom sometimes went mad.

Stokes materialised, delayed by having to load a film. He was too late. The sky had been wiped like a blackboard. 'At the Equator night falls fast,' Philip Grant informed him, unnecessarily.

Dinner was a strangely muted meal. In addition to their food the youngsters had a banquet of impressions to digest. But they stirred themselves during the second course. What nobody suspected was that the bunch of bananas at Maude Mimpriss's elbow harboured an uninvited guest. It - a hairy tarantula the diameter of a soup-plate - advanced diffidently over the white table-cloth. Too shocked to scream, she sat petrified. Susan and Vanessa, neither enamoured of spiders, pushed their chairs back sharply. The boys were hardly more composed - except Norman, who seemed genuinely curious. Ben Bellingham acted promptly. Manipulating a glass bowl and a tray, he imprisoned the intruder, and laboratory scientist Freddie Cairns was sent for. Relieved applause around the table.

In the small hours, while most slept, *Sea Shepherd* emerged from the Narrows...and out into the sweeping expanse of the river.

At ten o'clock next morning Susan led her class-mates to the stern. Ben was waiting. He held up crossed fingers. 'With a bit of luck I'll be able to complete my lecture. Trouble is, *where* to start? You met one local resident at dinner last night, a cuddly customer compared with the Brazilian wandering spider, most poisonous of all arachnids.'

Maude Mimpriss closed her eyes.

'Maybe you should follow Miss Mimpriss's example and close your eyes. It might help you to visualise the abundance of living things.

'In the river there are 2,000 fish species, with possibly another 1,000 to be identified - more than in the Atlantic, ten times more than in Europe's rivers. And in or around the forest are 900 bird species - including a hundred kinds of humming-bird; 95 reptile species; 46 species of bat - among them the vampire bat, inspiration

122

for radar; frogs as big as bulldog puppies; miniature marmosets; plants that cure leprosy and could combat cancer and Aids; 6,000 tree types - such as the Brazil nut tree, producing milk that is better for babies than cows' milk, and the copaiba which yields four gallons of diesel-like oil in a tapping, used instead of petrol for trucks...'

Ben broke off to gather his thoughts.

'A tenth of the world's bird species inhabit the Amazon. And what birds! The diminutive horned sungem, whose wings beat ninety times a second. The brilliant manakin - bouncing, cart-wheeling and dancing during courtship. The Andean condor...I know, I know, Norman, it's found on the *fringe* of the Amazon. But some neighbours warrant attention. So, the condor - all 25 pounds of it - can glide sixty miles on air currents with its ten-foot wings, can go without eating for forty days if it has to, but gorge 18 pounds of meat at a single sitting. It will even attack an ailing horse, and may reach the ripe old age of 72.'

Equally extraordinary: the fish. Ben elaborated. Lord of the freshwater fraternity is the pirarucu. Fifteen feet long, must surface regularly to breath. Then there's the aruana, which leaps high out of the water to snatch beetles from branches. And the tambaqui, 600-pound big brother of the piranha, with nut-cracking jaws. Related is the electric eel, capable of delivering a 650-volt charge (a household socket puts out 240 volts).

'Open your eyes now,' Ben said. 'Don't want you dropping off.' A remote risk, to judge from expressions. After describing an anaconda, the giant water snake that hugs crocodiles to death, he wound up the preliminary part of his lecture. 'Take a spin round the deck,' he advised, 'get some exercise. See you back here in quarter of an hour.'

Well before time, every seat was filled again. 'Thank you,' Ben said solemnly, resuming the lecture. 'Many of the creatures I've mentioned have a price on their furred, feathered or scaled heads.

'Each year the fashion industry demands 10 million reptile skins. They may be smuggled to Panama and shipped to Germany, France, Italy, Spain, Japan... It's a dirty business, with Mafia connections.

123

'Exotic birds - toucans, parrots, macaws - are persecuted too. Captured alive, those that don't starve or suffocate in transit often end up in private collections. Brazil's Spix's macaw, a blue-plumaged beauty, is now virtually extinct in the wild because the last nestlings have been taken.

'In certain places jaguar shoots are laid on for tourists...'

He stared at the deck. 'I sometimes think humanity has a suicidal streak. We slaughter each other, slaughter the animals and then, to finish the job, we try to put paid to the planet.'

As if to provide proof, dark clouds billowed from the distant bank. Smoke. 'By burning the trees - at up to an acre a second - man is literally playing with fire,' Ben declared.

Pacing back and forth, he continued: 'That sounds melodramatic, I know, but I'm not exaggerating. Rain forests are the cradle of our past, present and future. Covering just six per cent of all land, they contain well over half the species. Until recently botanists and biologists believed there were three million life forms, of which 1.6 million have been classified. Now it's thought there are 30 million species of tropical insect alone!'

He checked his watch.

'By 2050, assuming we survive, the human population will have doubled to 10.5 billion. Yet even today, one-fifth of us go hungry. The Amazon rain forest *could* supply at least a thousand plants for vegetable crops to boost the small number already cultivated. But...' Ben pointed to the drifting smoke.

'The deforestation of Amazonia - through ranching, road building, mining, oil drilling, logging, iron ore smelting - is an unparalleled crime against nature. Soil bakes tough as concrete. Rivers run foul with toxic substances.

'Take a long hard look, so you can tell your children what the jungle was like. Unless sanity prevails, this leafy luxuriance will become as desolate as a moonscape.'

Yves got to his feet. 'Excuse me, Ben. I don't mean to be rude, but surely the Brazilians and others won't listen to countries that don't practise what they preach? Besides, these schemes must

124

offer *some* advantages.'

Ben responded instantly. 'Advantages? Yes. Money, mainly, to make the rich richer. The poor, a vast majority, stay poor. And prowling gunmen - the notorious *pistoleiros* - are hired to "take care of" anybody who doesn't co-operate.'

He drew nearer. 'My answer over-simplifies the problem, which is complicated by foreign debts. But no nation has the right to destroy an asset vital to the health of the whole planet. You see, Yves, the few advantages are outweighed by one disadvantage. It's a dreadful disadvantage. And it's this: if we lose the rain forests, as we could by the year 2020, a billion-plus people who depend on them for water will be enduring hellish conditions. By then, of course, the world's weather would have gone completely haywire.'

Yves didn't speak again.

Ben puffed out his cheeks. 'Which brings me to *the* hottest ecological topic - global warming, result of the greenhouse effect.'

Rapidly he summarised the unwelcome facts. Forty gases are steadily building up in the atmosphere to trap the sun's heat and raise temperatures. The principal culprit: carbon dioxide (CO_2), a by-product of the fossil fuels coal and oil.

'Trees absorb CO_2. By felling the forests, man is removing an essential air-filter. Burning them releases even more of the gas. It's a vicious circle,' said Ben, 'and I mean vicious.'

Another glance at his watch. 'So what can humanity look forward to? Worse and wider-spread droughts, floods, famine, hurricanes far fiercer than Hannah. And God knows what else.

'The most disturbing prospect is a rise in sea-levels as polar ice-caps melt. A 26-foot rise, according to the gloomiest prophecy. If warming isn't halted, much of our coastal land will be inundated during the next century - and some of the world's major cities...'

Susan mumbled in Gary's ear: 'Don't fancy scuba-diving to the shops.' His own mind was awash with images of London under water.

Ben had moved on. 'To absorb the annual output of man-made CO_2,' he was saying, 'we'd need to plant a forest twice the size of

125

Australia. And that's at today's rate. Thirty years from now, developing countries like China and India could be adding as much again to the CO2 total. Together we've got to beat this environmental crisis.'

Half to herself, Vanessa remarked: 'Seems hopeless.' In the silence, she blushed.

'Not quite,' Ben pointed out. 'We *can* change, find solutions. Use less coal and oil, for instance. Harness wind, solar and tidal power. Protect and extend the forests.

'However, let's suppose we do nothing. What then? I suspect our weakened world will heal itself - and the cure would be drastic. Planet Earth will keep revolving and life will go on. But not necessarily human life.

'Mankind, I believe, has a choice: either act responsibly or perish. If we perish, maybe we deserve to.'

A final glance at his watch.

'And here - forgive the gaps - I must end my lecture. It won't be long before you're in the jungle,' Ben reminded them, 'experiencing for yourselves. See you later. Ah, I almost forgot. Details of the essay competition based on your field-work. I think you'll approve of the prize.'

Geoffrey Baggalley handed out envelopes.

11 Face to face

The radio room door wouldn't open. Leslie Curtis barged against it; bounced back, rubbing his shoulder. 'Bloody thing's jammed,' he muttered, 'can't be locked.'

From a recess in the corridor, partly concealed by shadow, Darren delighted in this performance like a toddler at the circus. Except that he dare not call out. Curtis the clown merited a wider public.

Darren was convinced his thoughts had travelled when James Alexander marched past and up to the perturbed radio officer.

'Mr. Curtis, I need to speak to London.'

'Of course, Captain, but there's a temporary problem.'

Darren's signal brought Norman from another hiding-place. Nonchalantly he rambled towards the radio room.

'The door's locked itself,' Alexander said, 'and the key's inside. Have I got it right?'

Behind them Norman bent to tie his shoe-lace.

'Borrow Philip Grant's master-key,' the captain commanded tersely.

On deck, for the first time in many hours, Ben Bellingham filled his lungs with Amazonian air and listened to the rippling river. Manaus was not far off. He shifted position. Since the lecture, days ago, he'd been compelled to neglect the students.

Ben felt regret - followed, unaccountably, by a sense of

foreboding. Why? Memory gave him the reason: *We'll meet again, Bellingham. And then you die.* A crook's cheap talk? It could cost Ben dear to find out...

On the opposite side of the ship, Darren and Norman were jostled by clustering companions. 'Don't keep us in suspense,' Vanessa pleaded. For once Norman was speechless - the limelight belonged to Darren. With glowing satisfaction he related every move in the radio room farce. Then, delving into his trouser pocket, he produced a key. A skeleton key. 'My dad's. Knew it'd come in handy.' They all stared down at his palm. 'That's just where I've got Curtis.'

Now Norman butted in, though not to remark on Darren's exploits. 'Look, the river! Have you ever seen anything like it?'

A collective rush to the rail.

Susan's mouth formed a perfectly round O. 'It's striped, two-tone. Ben...Ben...'

Clearing his troubled mind, he answered the excited summons. 'Ah, the Wedding of the Waters. I wondered when you'd notice. Black and white coffee flowing side by side. The dark water enters from the Negro, a tributary, but doesn't merge with the paler Amazon for miles.'

On the bridge a pilot yawned, his navigation duties nearly over. *Sea Shepherd* altered course, branching off into the Negro.

What an anticlimax! Gary's reaction to a sprawl of industrial structures and a power-station belching fumes. Manaus, jewel of the jungle?

In 1900 Manaus had been a world centre, a kind of Eldorado where fabulous fortunes were made. Rubber, rather than gold, was the source of this wealth; an exclusive gift from the jungle trees. But Manaus's rubber boom ceased when seeds were 'smuggled' out and plantations established in Asia.

Sea Shepherd docked...in a floating harbour, which rises and falls with the wet and dry seasons.

Most passengers took a guided tour of the city, at least as bustling as Belem. Office blocks, well-stocked shops, get-out-of-my-way traffic. However, here and there, more ornate architecture - notably the magnificent opera-house - hinted at bygone glory.

Their tour done, all returned to *Sea Shepherd*. Just time for a cool cabin shower and a bite to eat before disembarking again. A grey coach stood ready on the quay, idly observed by loafers.

As the coach pulled away, the loafers dispersed. With the exception of one man, a scar-faced man. He spat.

The National Institute for Amazon Research, five miles out of town, is not as grand as it sounds. An informal arrangement of low wooden buildings in forest that peeps from every side. Flags hung on tall poles: the Brazilian flag, the flag of the State of Amazonas and, in honour of Ben Bellingham and company, the Union Jack. Crossing the campus, the visitors were introduced to ethnobotanists. 'Scientists who study how tribal people use plants as medicine,' Yves translated. 'Correct,' Norman conceded.

These new acquaintances, destined to become trusted friends - Vanessa had already picked her favourite - would lead teams on far-ranging expeditions.

Later, aboard *Sea Shepherd,* Gary and Susan lingered over dinner. 'Prob'ly the last decent grub we'll get for weeks.' He was thinking of the jungle safaris, due to depart at dawn. Who'd be going where and with whom? Susan and Gary...together or apart?

Morning, five o'clock. Susan fastened the straps of her bulging rucksack and laid it on the bunk. Wails from a not-yet-dressed Vanessa. 'Too much stuff. Boots, bath-cap, beastly insect repellent! There's no space for my clothes. And I must take shampoo... Help me pack, please.' Susan weeded out the inessential items; first, a cosmetics case. 'You get dressed, I'll finish off.'

They descended the gangway to a quay wreathed in rosy mist. The party was complete. Susan swallowed hard - she and Gary had been assigned to different teams. But not permanently.

Each group began to assume an independence, each contemplating the great road and river journeys ahead.

After one week, Gary and Yves regarded themselves as veteran explorers. They wore the badges of their apprenticeship - scabs, scratches, insect bites - with manly pride. Maude Mimpriss, less stoical, was tolerated and frequently teased. A beefy German named Helmut (Vanessa's favourite) presided over the threesome and, without seeming to, imposed a necessary discipline. Helmut spoke English well.

Venturing into the jungle, the boys had known only vaguely what to expect. Not an animal reception committee; surely, though, some creature would deign to put in an appearance. Nothing. Neither parrot nor monkey anywhere. But you could hear them, like musical instruments being tuned.

Helmut, dripping in the sauna-bath atmosphere, pointed upwards with a machete. 'That is where most live. At three levels.' Trees of varying height create distinct layers, which house separate communities. The canopy layer at 100 to 130 feet, he explained, is the most densely populated. 'Sloths, snakes, eagles, cats...all co-existing in a twenty-foot-thick habitat.'

Mimpriss tripped on a tree root, one of dozens wriggling across the forest floor. Gary and Yves hauled her up. They were getting used to the daytime twilight, growing more observant. It would have been a pity to miss seeing the myriad leaf-cutter ants, each bearing a leaf fragment aloft like a banner. 'Everything here is recycled fast,' said Helmut.

As time passed, the team adapted to a strict schedule. Up at 5.30 a.m, back in hammocks by 8.00 p.m.

Mint-fresh mornings, sweltering afternoons, chilly nights. Gary and Yves had lots to discuss: the red-crested lizard, a basilisk, scampering upright on two large flat feet over the surface of a secluded stream...a crocodile skeleton picked gleaming white by piranhas...torrents, ripped by rocky rapids or tumbling from on high in rainbow-straddled waterfalls...

Maude Mimpriss matched their wonderment, which surprised the boys. And they surprised themselves by liking her more and more. But that didn't stop the teasing.

One evening, as Helmut tended the cooking fire under a magnified moon, Yves and Gary 'entertained' her with true tales of eighteen-inch leeches and blood-sucking bats. She shuddered. Helmut grinned and dished out the food, a rather dreary diet based on provisions brought by boat and supplemented with forest produce. However, none of the three complained. Helmut served up mugs of tea and - from a hitherto absent tin - '*Kuchen*. German cake. You will enjoy'.

They retired to their hammocks, strung between trees and sheltered by palm fronds. Beneath the mosquito-net, Gary tried to envisage Susan's day. How she would have gobbled up Helmut's cake! Ku... Kuchen.

During the night he was woken by a yell. Yves. A rope supporting his hammock had parted. The work of some sharp-toothed rodent - or Mimpriss's revenge? While Gary shone a torch, Helmut spliced the rope and did repairs that he hoped would hold till dawn. Soon all were asleep again.

Before they broke camp next morning, Yves sounded another alarm. Near him leaves were rustling.

A dog-like head came softly to rest on the ground. Above, secured by the tail to a branch, stretched fifteen feet of supple body. Unwinding its tail, the boa constrictor performed an unbelievable balancing act, standing in a muscular column, defying gravity. Mesmerised, Yves and Gary watched the brown-patterned body 'flow' slowly down.

With weaving grace the snake went on its way.

Helmut told them how Indian villagers keep young boas as pets to dispose of rats, mice and bats. 'It is the second biggest Amazonian snake. The anaconda is the biggest. No one would make a pet of an anaconda. No one...'

*

131

Far from Gary, though not in spirit, Susan was astir too. She tiptoed past the sagging hammocks and still-snoozing occupants. Alone! Her and the jungle. By the river, birds hurled streamers of song from highlighted treetops. Closer, a brrrr-ing, like Morse code. Must be a woodpecker.

Spreading her cardigan on a dewy log, Susan sat and flicked through her notebook. Plenty there, but which bits shall I use in my essay? She started to read.

Juan, our nice Brazilian ethno, says an Indian child has 50 names for a bee. Yet an insectologist was unable to distinguish between certain species without examining them in the Institute lab. 'Indians, primitive? They could teach us a thing or two.'

Over a quarter of all medicines are derived from rain forest plants. 'Yes, but how much more is going up in smoke? Five times as much? I'll have to check with Juan.'

Humming-birds can fly backwards, and they build their nests partly from spiders' webs. 'Spiders' webs. Clever. I bet Norman doesn't know that.'

'I do.' Norman's voice, behind her.

Susan shot into the air. 'You...you... Scared the daylights out of me. You've got less common sense than this log. And why don't you mind your own business?'

Norman wisely avoided an argument. Straightening his glasses, he said: 'Breakfast is ready.'

Susan sulked throughout the meal, barely responding to a polite inquiry from the fourth member of the team - Peter Stokes. Afterwards, as Juan led them off, she was acutely aware of Norman following in her footsteps.

Juan helped each into the moored canoe and roused the outboard motor. In such vastness, wooded and watery, the craft seemed very small.

During a break for lunch, Norman mystified the men with card tricks. Susan, despite herself, was captivated. Norman 'plucked' a joker from the pack. She didn't look away but jabbed him in the stomach: an ungentle gesture of forgiveness.

132

The overcast sky made her suddenly homesick for England. Don't rain... How silly! Dry season or not, a rain forest ought to be - well - rainy.

By four o'clock it *was*. A perpetual bombardment from bulging clouds. Juan had deciphered the omens. Before the first rumble, he steered for the bank. His general dislike of machines turned into something stronger when the motor coughed and cut out. They were adrift. Susan and Norman donned wet-weather gear; Stokes, scrabbling in his rucksack, uncovered a box of dominoes and the trusty calculator...but no raincoat.

It was then that the purple heavens opened and a deluge beat down on them, pitting the water like pellets, threatening to swamp the boat. While Juan cussed and tinkered, the others frantically bailed or paddled. Beyond, the jungle was being bleached by lightning.

Rrrrum...rrrrum. Juan took the tiller again and got them to land. Eventually the rain relented.

They camped early at a new site, and Juan somehow kindled a blaze. Peter Stokes, sodden and snuffly, crouched almost on top of it.

After eating, Susan delayed her date with the hammock. She could have stood for hours gazing up at the litter of stars - if Juan had let her. He didn't.

Rocking herself to sleep, she dreamt that a jaguar lay by their all-night camp-fire, warming its spotted bulk like any hearth-side moggie.

Juan brewed morning coffee. Nobody appreciated it more than Stokes. 'I'm an idiot, fancy leaving my raincoat aboard *Sea Shepherd!*' His glance strayed to the shirt he'd draped, airing, on a bush. 'Oh, no...' It was unrecognisable. Scraps, a few buttons. 'Leaf-cutter ants,' Juan pronounced. He maintained a deadpan expression - too great an effort for Susan and Norman.

From now on they would spend their days with the Indians. Page after page of Susan's notebook was given over to descriptions and drawings of village huts, painted bodies, unusual foods and proud hunters bearing blowpipes.

Juan had rightly said that the Indians live in the Stone Age *and* the 20th century. Ancient traditions combined with modern technology; feathers and beads for some, snazzy shirts and shorts for others.

Koita, the village shaman or healer, wore a red loin-cloth and ear-rings. Susan showed him instant respect; not because of his seniority - he was 70 - but because he obviously deserved it.

Shamans such as Koita, dotted across Amazonia, are a vanishing breed. They alone know and can unlock the 'magic' in each plant. That knowledge, not written down, will pass away with them. They have no successors. Which is why ethnobotanists, racing against the clock and forest fires, are trying to record as much as possible.

Did plant constituents really cure snakebites, make you lose weight, promote fertility? Susan accepted it, Norman was dubious.

But later, hollering from wasp stings, he changed his mind. Koita rubbed a ground-up leaf on Norman's skin. Within five minutes the pain had gone - and any sign that he'd been stung.

When the time came to leave the Indians for good, Koita offered Susan a job as his assistant. Whether or not the medicine-man was serious, Susan believed she would never be paid a finer compliment.

Meanwhile, what of the third party: Darren, Vanessa, Baggalley and their leader, Brad? At first both students treated each other with reserve. Too dissimilar to be natural buddies. And neither could quite forget Darren's thieving.

However, weeks of joint endeavour, pleasures, hardships and occasional laughter brought the pair closer to affection. Deprived of make-up, with unkempt hair and broken fingernails, Vanessa looked decidedly unglamorous. Darren found he preferred her that way. She preferred *him* to his usual self.

He was keeping a detailed list of every animal sighted.

Although Darren hadn't actually seen a vampire bat, he had received a visit from one. At midnight, appropriately. If not for a warm trickle of blood down his arm - protruding from the mosquito-net - he might have slept on unaware.

By firelight Brad applied iodine to the wound and bound it tightly. The American spoke in unflattering terms about vampire habits. 'An evil guy, like something hatched by Satan. Only three inches of 'im, but he can do a lotta damage. Two long incisors to chisel holes, and saliva that contains an anaesthetic and anti-clotting agent.'

Would Darren add the vampire to his list?

He would certainly include four giant otters - rare Amazon residents - which the group came across on a languid afternoon. The experience was to affect him deeply.

It all began with a muffled bang. A gunshot? Brad strode out to investigate, ordering the others to stay well back. Vanessa and Darren disobeyed, arriving at the river bank as Brad drew near to a startled peasant. In his right hand, a rifle. In his left, a net stuffed and straining with captive cubs. Beside him, the seven-foot corpse of an adult otter.

Vanessa reacted instinctively, running forward. 'Let them go!' Darren joined her. Brad and Baggalley were too slow to intervene. The peasant, puzzled and defensive, tightened his grip on the gun. 'Let them go...please.' Vanessa undid her wrist-watch. 'I'll give you this.' The peasant took it and dropped the net. Grabbing the dead otter's tail, he beat a retreat.

'Forgive me, Mother,' Vanessa said tearfully. 'I know you'd understand.'

With Geoffrey Baggalley's aid, Brad released the cubs. A scream rent the air. Another fully-grown otter was lolloping towards the cubs. 'Let's get out of here, pronto!' Brad urged. 'Unless you wanna lose a limb.'

His object achieved, he wagged an admonishing finger at the teenagers. 'Do as I say in future.' Vanessa wept. 'OK,' Brad sighed. 'As a conservationist what you did was kind and brave. Too brave.'

Darren kept very quiet. Guilt, shame, sympathy were swirling in his mind. Vanessa's watch, that meant so much to her, sacrificed!

The watch he had robbed her of. Just as he'd taken the pennant from his otter-loving friend, Rhonda. He *must* make amends, and soon.

For Ben Bellingham, today would also prove fateful - perhaps fatal. But, so far, there was no hint of this.

Leaving the field station, Ben whistled as he walked a leafy path between machete-marked trees. Surely The Eden Mission could spare him for a while.

He reached the river. Removing his hat, he halted.

'Bellingham!'

Ben twisted, heart hammering. Close behind him, a black-clad figure. Where had he come from? Ben focused on the face: scarred cheek, penetrating eyes. Then he saw the knife.

'Who are you?' Ben demanded. 'What do you want?'

The man grinned insolently, in no hurry to reply. He was revelling in the situation.

Ben racked his brain. The scarred face. Familiar? Yes - on the quay at Manaus. But that wasn't all. He recollected the trial, the description of the trawler hijacker. It fitted...him. *And then you die.*

'You know me now, Bellingham? Uh?' The blade glinted.

'Not your name or why you're doing this.'

'It is safe to tell you - I am Mendoza. And why I kill you? Because I am paid, because you are in the way, because I like to.'

Suddenly he lunged.

Pivoting, Ben deflected the thrust with his canvas shoulder-bag. Mendoza circled, grinning. He charged in again, and the silver blade slashed. Ben gasped. His wrist bubbled red. He swung the bag wildly. It caught in a branch. Defenceless! Flinging aside his hat, he squared up like a prize-fighter, before backing away...only to stumble.

Mendoza pounced, but Ben's fingers closed on a lump of wood. As his adversary stooped to finish the job, Ben clubbed him.

Mendoza pitched forward, dazed. Ben rolled, then struggled to his feet - the unlikeliest of victors. However, celebration was premature.

Mendoza's mad eyes were staring at him, their lethal message reinforced by the revolver in his hand.

And there it should have ended.

Neither man had seen the anaconda cruising through the water or ascending the bank. An olive-green gargantuan intent on feeding. Mendoza shrieked as six sets of teeth buried themselves in his neck. It was the last sound he ever made. The 35-foot snake whipped its coils around him in a suffocating crush. Ben's heroic efforts to stage a rescue were thwarted by the reptile's lashing tail. In any case, it was too late.

Falling to his knees, he saw the anaconda take Mendoza's head into its own.

12 Curtis

Ben...in hospital. He'd outmanoeuvred an assassin. *Sea Shepherd* hummed with rumours, embellished by each telling.

Of the students, Susan and Vanessa were most worried about his welfare. How badly hurt was he? Would he get better soon? And when would he be back among them? But to the others, Ben now seemed invincible.

He probably hoped for a discreet return to ship - no fuss - and to resume work at once. Not likely, under the circumstances. Even James Alexander's obsession with finding the saboteur temporarily abated. Ben was on his way! From bridge and engine-room, galley and laboratory, well-wishers converged near the top of the gangway.

'There he is!' Susan squeaked.

A law officer accompanied him. Limping slightly and with his arm in a sling, Ben peered up at the uneven line of faces and waved his free hand. *Sea Shepherd* sounded a siren salute as he mounted the gangway. The police inspector or *delegado,* a short, moustached man, boarded too.

Clapping and cheering.

Johnny Masterson thumped Ben's shoulder. He grimaced. 'Go easy on me, still a bit sore.'

The *delegado* waited patiently for several minutes, then announced: '*Senhor* Bellingham, I am going to your captain's cabin. Please come, and we will try to conclude this distressing affair.'

Around Ben the crowd thinned to six. Boldly Vanessa stretched

138

and gave him a kiss. Norman had appointed himself spokesman. 'We're just grateful you're here, because you *are*...The Eden Mission.'

Ben cleared his throat. 'Well, life's full of surprises and not always unpleasant. It's so nice to see you all again. Now then, what about those essays? Finished yet? I need a good read.'

With feelings they couldn't express, they watched him hobble off.

Next, a get-together in Yves and Darren's cabin. 'Poor Ben,' said Susan, 'he looks ill.' Gary agreed. Norman and Yves started to talk at the same time.

'Do shut up!' Darren, squatting on his bunk, cut in with a newly acquired directness. 'Yap, yap, yap. We've got more important stuff to discuss. Curtis - remember?'

No one contradicted him.

Vanessa: 'I wonder. You know what happened to Ben. Could Curtis be involved?'

Darren: 'I wouldn't put it past him, the rat.' Abruptly he stood. Crossing to the cupboard, he dug out the packet. Every eye was on him as he tore it open.

'Stop!' Susan looked frightened. 'Darren, don't you realise...?'

'Yeah, I realise a lot. I've done some pretty rotten things - stealing and lying. Maybe it wasn't all my fault, but I've got to change. Or - Curtis wins.'

'And your dad?' Gary put the crucial question.

'He told me to stick up for myself, used to say bullies are really cowards.'

Sunlight slanted through the porthole. The black book gleamed invitingly.

Darren didn't resist.

In Alexander's cabin, the *delegado* placed two objects side by side on the desk. 'The weapons,' he said simply. Ben, who had seen them before, showed less interest than either the captain or Masterson.

'The knife, *senhores*, is the trademark of Carlos Mendoza. Note the notches on the handle. Eight notches, eight murders. And yours, *Senhor* Bellingham, would have been the ninth.'

Ben sat down.

'You OK?' Masterson checked. Ben nodded.

The *delegado* continued: 'Now to the gun. It did not belong to Mendoza. It belonged to - a friend of mine. A policeman, Miguel Osuna. I sometimes visit his widow and children...

'We never recovered Miguel's body, but this revolver is proof enough.

'Justice. How strange! For years Mendoza defied it. And then an anaconda carries out the death penalty.'

Back in the boys' cabin. *Carlos Mendoza, hired killer for Maximilian Kruger*. The black book entry leapt from the page. 'Mendoza!' Darren exclaimed. 'Isn't that...' he recalled the rumours '...the name of the man who tried to murder Ben?'

A half-gasp from Susan.

The book had yielded ample information - names, business interests, connections. An international syndicate, pursuing partly or wholly criminal activities on a scale quite beyond the teenagers' comprehension. But the reference to Mendoza was more easily understood. It linked Curtis to this network.

'As good as a signed confession!' Darren was grimly exultant.

Norman: 'So what's our next move, Darren?'

'I'm going to give the book to Ben.'

Vanessa: 'What'll you tell him?'

'The truth - about a saboteur who just happens to have the name of Ben's attacker written down in black and white.'

With a trace of embarrassment, Yves pointed out: 'Ben's bound to ask how you got the book, why Curtis chose you. Which will lead on to other things...like your, um, kleptomania.'

An uneasy hush enfolded them. Darren held his head in his hands. Eventually Gary spoke up: 'We're with you all the way.' Norman added: 'Your probation's over.'

On deck, the *delegado* took his leave of Alexander. '*Adeus,* Captain, safe voyage!' Shortly afterwards *Sea Shepherd* set sail -

140

for Antarctica.

By the time Alexander returned to his cabin, Ben had summoned and fully briefed the teachers. Maude Mimpriss was in a motherly mood. 'You must rest, Ben. Otherwise you'll suffer and so will The Eden Mission. What do you think, Captain Alexander?'

'Couldn't agree more. In fact, I insist he takes a break. If necessary I'll use the anchor chain to tie him down!'

Ben shrugged, wishing he hadn't as the pain throbbed.

A timid knock at the door.

Alexander: 'Someone see who that is.' Baggalley tugged the handle smartly. Darren almost fell into him, closely followed by Susan and troupe. Darren blurted: 'We - I - need to talk to Ben. Urgently.'

'Sorry. Not now, I'm afraid.' Baggalley was emphatic.

But Ben prevailed. 'Let 'em in.'

Exposed to the adults' view, Darren lost his tongue. Ben smiled. 'Say your piece, son, I'm listening.'

Darren hesitated. 'It's, er, sort of confidential, if you know what I mean.'

Lethargically Ben lifted himself from the chair. 'Let's go outside.'

In the corridor he kept his promise and listened. Until then he'd thought events had made him shock-proof. Nonplussed, he questioned Darren. 'Are you *certain?* These are very serious allegations.' A chorus of confirmation. Darren thrust the black book at Ben, drawing attention to the most incriminating entry. Ben leaned against a bulkhead. 'Incredible! You did right to come to me, Darren.' He ushered them into the adjoining cabin and told them to stay put. 'I'll be back in a while.'

For half an hour, Alexander's cabin resounded to intermittent utterances of astonishment and anger. Assessing each page, Ben spotted *Anilux*, an old foe. And he was more than intrigued by a schedule of his movements near Santa Barbara. A blueprint for the ramming.

Suddenly it all began to make sense, sickening sense. The kidnap attempt...the sabotage...the submariners' fate...the worldwide

141

disruption of conservation projects...

'Good God!' Ben paled. 'Curtis is perfectly positioned to feed out classified data to our enemies. It's at his fingertips, literally.

'Their own agent in our midst, at Mission HQ, the nerve-centre. Clever. No wonder they're always one jump ahead. Who knows what harm he's done? We can guess from some of the reports.'

James Alexander erupted. 'I want that traitor off my ship!'

Masterson: 'He ought to be held here and thoroughly interrogated.'

Alexander restrained his rage, conscious that Masterson had a point - and that *Sea Shepherd* could be delayed for months once the Brazilian authorities were brought in.

Recovering his self-control, the captain spoke again: 'Mr. Masterson, we have a distasteful task to perform.'

Peter Stokes rose. 'Geoffrey and I were half-way through a game of dominoes, perhaps we can finish it now?' Maude, also uncomfortable at this stage, mentioned: 'And I've lessons to prepare.'

Abstracted, the captain did not even acknowledge their departure. Ben went next door, leaving Alexander and Masterson to act.

Ben's brief appearance failed to allay the students' restlessness. 'The captain can't see you yet, it shouldn't be much longer.' Only Gary and Vanessa, chatting quietly in a corner, seemed not to mind the wait. Susan found it harder and harder to pretend she didn't feel jealous.

In the radio room, Curtis was taken unawares, his back to the door. 'What the blazes! Bursting in like that!' He assumed a respectful expression. 'Ah, Captain, it's you. And Mr. Masterson. How can I help?'

Alexander jerked his thumb like a hitch-hiker. 'To my cabin. Immediately.'

'But who'll man the radio?'

'A trustworthy deputy.'

'Why? Is there an emergency?'

'You'd relish it, wouldn't you?'

The respectful expression vanished. 'What are you getting at?'

142

'Sabotage. Now, move!'

Ben was already seated when they arrived. Curtis and Masterson remained standing, Alexander went directly to his desk. In clinical tones he read out the charges. Predictably Curtis denied everything and declared himself baffled; he'd been framed, victimised, made a scapegoat.

Ben had heard enough. Brandishing the book, he advanced on Curtis. 'Save your breath - you can't explain this away.'

The radio officer grunted. 'Am I supposed to know what that is?'

Ben rubbed his eyes. 'I'm tired, Curtis. Tired of having my work undone, tired of dodging killers, tired of you.' He tapped the book. 'You're as guilty as they are.'

Curtis blustered for a few seconds, then cracked. Defeated by months of pressure - and damning evidence. His confession came quickly.

Without looking up, as though he couldn't endure the sight of him, Alexander pronounced: 'You are relieved of duties and will be confined to quarters under guard.' He reached for the intercom on his desk. 'I'll arrange an escort.'

A cowed Curtis interjected: 'There's no need, I won't cause trouble. I'll tell you whatever you want. Let's just...get the record straight.' Alexander removed his finger from the button. Curtis kept talking. 'The organization spares *nobody*. The book was my insurance policy. But now, my days are numbered.'

Ben attracted the captain's attention. 'The students, Jim. When?' Alexander considered. 'Tomorrow, early.' With no regrets Bellingham left.

'Tomorrow!' Darren stared miserably at Ben. 'Yes, you'll just have to sweat it out.' By chance, they emerged into the corridor at the same moment as Masterson and Curtis. Darren nearly choked. Curbing the instinct to run, he stood his ground and braced himself for, at the very least, a verbal assault. However, when Curtis did speak it was in a sneering undertone: 'Stupid kid. We couldn't have touched your father.'

He turned to Masterson. 'Mind if I smoke?'

Dad, safe! Darren rejoiced silently. His next thought was less pleasing. He'd been duped.

Curtis had found his cigarettes but no lighter.

'Try your top-right pocket,' Darren suggested.

The lighter was there. Curtis blinked, then glowered with all his old menace, stung by the memory of too many humiliations. 'So it *was* you...playing dirty tricks!'

Yves, not Darren, made the obvious retort: 'You're a fine one to talk!'

Ben broke up what might have developed into a slanging match. 'That'll do.'

Gripping Curtis's arm, Masterson steered him towards the spare cabin - sparsely furnished and without a porthole. His cell for the remainder of the voyage.

Sea Shepherd's engines drummed through another Amazon day. Dusk. On deck, Gary tried to embrace Susan. She side-stepped, in a huff. 'What will your sweetheart say?' Gary was taken aback. 'My what?' 'Your girlfriend - *Vain*essa.' He gestured, exasperated. 'You're being silly.' 'No I'm not. I saw you together, behaving as if I didn't exist.' 'I was only giving her some advice about her essay.' 'Pah! Can't you do better than that?' Susan flounced off.

Later, undressing for bed, she muttered insults at the bathroom door. Behind it Vanessa was preening in the mirror. Susan hurled a pillow across the cabin.

In her own good time Vanessa reappeared, resembling a model from a toothpaste commercial.

'Is anything the matter, Susan? You seem rather broody.'

Susan didn't want to reply, nor did she. She looked down at her bunk, to the space where the pillow had been. A small red box lay there. 'This yours?' she asked curtly, eyes still averted.

'No, not mine.'

Frowning, Susan lifted the lid and unwrapped some tissue-paper

- to reveal a gold locket and chain. She unfastened the catch. Inside, a colour photograph of her and Gary.

She swung sideways to face Vanessa. 'How did it get there?' Vanessa's smile broadened. 'Guess. I wish someone loved me that much.'

Susan took her hand. 'So you and Gary aren't...?'

'Listen, Gary's great. But he's *your* boyfriend.'

Feeling foolish, repentant and happy, Susan willed away the hours till morning.

At breakfast she learned that Gary had bought the gift in Manaus and recruited Vanessa to 'plant' it. Susan smothered him with affection. 'Sorry I doubted you, but you almost made me jealous.' Gary kept mischievously mum.

Opposite, Darren was also quiet - though for totally different reasons. Very soon he must justify himself to Captain Alexander. His heart pattered as Ben approached.

Outside Alexander's cabin, Ben told Darren and the others what to expect.

Gruffly the captain received them. Then, with Ben and Johnny Masterson, he sat back to hear Darren's account.

That account left out no detail of his shameful past, his collaboration with Curtis or why it had occurred. At the end of what was a courageous speech, Darren stepped forward and passed over to Alexander a bundle of dollar bills - 'wages' from Curtis. 'I haven't spent any.'

'Tell me,' Alexander inquired, 'what's the pay for aiding and abetting a saboteur, cheating on your friends? You're a disgrace - and a fool. I can't think of a single reason why you shouldn't be sent home.'

Impulsively Susan protested: 'That's unfair. Darren couldn't help doing what he did. And it's thanks to him you caught Curtis.'

James Alexander regarded her frostily. 'When I want your opinion, young lady, I'll ask for it.' He rose, adding: 'To a certain extent you're all to blame.'

Ben's turn. 'I can understand why they kept their secret, Jim.

Besides, would you have believed them - about Curtis?'

Encouraged by this, Norman joined in. 'It's true. Our word against an officer's. We had no proof, not until Darren opened the packet.'

Alexander paced from behind his desk, nearer to Darren. 'Why wasn't I informed of your kleptomania before the voyage? Eh?'

Darren, earlier so articulate, floundered. 'My mother...I...you'd have stopped me coming.'

'Yes, I would,' Alexander admitted. He resumed his seat and conferred with Ben and Masterson. Gary winked at Darren, whose shirt was sticking to him.

The captain coughed, his decision made. 'Your conduct, to say the least, has left a lot to be desired. But you've got guts, lad, I'll give you that - and one more chance. *Don't* disappointment me!'

Darren's spontaneous reaction was to salute. 'No, sir!'

A whoop from Yves as Darren was mobbed.

Their voices echoing along the corridor, the teenagers went gladly to lessons. Before entering the lecture hall, Gary gave Susan a squeeze. 'Quite bright, aren't you?' he said. 'You mistrusted Curtis from the very beginning.'

For several days, while *Sea Shepherd* drew ever nearer to the Atlantic, Johnny Masterson spent time in the uncongenial company of Curtis. Cooped up, with guards outside. But Masterson was making progress, assembling facts that might be used to counter the organization.

How did Curtis, a minor syndicate employee, know so much? He bragged of having many sources. 'Chauffeurs, secretaries, people their bosses treat like dirt. And I learned a lot from the odd bit of computer-hacking.'

Masterson was impressed. He leafed through the black book, pausing at an entry in capital letters. 'Who's Rod Garston?' he queried. Curtis's confidence waned. Absurdly, as if afraid of being overheard, he whispered: 'The Director's personal trouble-shooter.'

146

'What does this Rod Garston look like?' 'Dunno - and I hope I never find out.'

Curtis refused to say more on the subject. However, he did confide that he had once feverishly imagined Garston stealing aboard at night. 'I even thought he'd searched my cabin. Should've realised it was those snotty-nosed brats.'

After the latest session with Curtis, Masterson conveyed his findings to a busy Alexander.

Dinner that evening had a special flavour, added spice. Not because of the food but because of an announcement Ben would make. *Ting. Ting. Ting.* Spoon and glass called a halt to every conversation. Ben stood, no longer wearing his sling. 'Thank you for your attention. It is my pleasant duty to declare the results of the essay competition. The judges - Maude Mimpriss, Geoffrey Baggalley, Peter Stokes and I - offer congratulations to all six students for work of an exceptionally high standard. Each of you can be proud.'

From under the table, Ben produced a copy of *Conservation,* the magazine that regularly featured his articles. 'The winner's essay will appear in the next issue.

'So, *who* is it? A very difficult choice. But the panel is unanimous...Darren!'

Noisy and prolonged applause. Flabbergasted, cheeks burning, Darren walked up to collect a cash prize of £500.

He examined his shoes as Ben heaped praise on him. The essay was 'a model of clear thinking and deep feeling, expressed in a style that bowled your teachers over. Miss Mimpriss, in particular, expects more from you in future.'

Darren relaxed a little at the general laughter, until Ben insisted on quoting the final paragraph from the essay: *Like a tolerant parent, the Earth has permitted us to misbehave, sometimes wildly. But it has been warning us to mend our ways. Dare we go on disobeying, draining every last drop of tolerance? If we do, the punishment will be almighty. And for ever.*

Darren, still shaken, rejoined his friends - and pressed the prize-money into Vanessa's hand. 'You keep it, divide it with the others.' Before she could dissent he was gone.

Soon *Sea Shepherd* would dock to load fresh supplies, ready for an Antarctic odyssey.

13 Last frontier

Hamburg. From the cruising Mercedes, Maximilian Kruger made a transatlantic phone call to Houston. 'Yup.' Art Benton. Without preliminaries, Kruger demanded: 'What's going on? I haven't heard from Curtis for over a week. Have you?'

'No, Max, I haven't.'

'I don't suppose it occurred to you his cover has been blown.'

'It did, but...'

'Does The Director know?'

'No. I'll speak to him.'

'Do it. Right away.'

'Look here, Max...'

Kruger rang off.

Benton shook his head. 'One day, you arrogant slob, you'll go too far.'

Maybe I *should* have phoned Zurich earlier, he thought. Apprehensively he dialled the private number. Before Benton had finished relating the news he was cut short by The Director. 'Do not concern yourself further. The matter will be dealt with. I suggest you and Kruger keep in closer contact; he reported this to me yesterday.'

Benton replaced the receiver slowly. 'Get me a drink,' he snapped at his secretary, 'and block all calls. No more interruptions - from anyone.'

*

By now, steaming south, *Sea Shepherd* had put a thousand briny miles astern. To starboard, the Brazilian coast would eventually give way to that of Uruguay, then Argentina. Then...out into Antarctic waters and on to an ice-capped continent, as big as China and India combined, clinging to the bottom of the globe.

Gary and Susan strolled in step across the deck. Both felt a kind of sadness, and wondered why. Because Amazonia was *behind* them? Because, soon, the voyage must end? He squeezed her hand. 'There's still Antarctica before we head home.'

On the bridge, Ben grinned crookedly. 'Never knew you had such a devious mind, Jim.' Beside him Johnny Masterson mulled over the captain's plan - use Curtis to transmit bogus 'news' to the organization. 'It's worth a try,' said Johnny. 'I'll tell Curtis he's got his job back, but working for us!'

On deck, Susan and Gary paused by an off-duty Philip Grant stretched out in a chair near the bow. 'Of course you're not intruding,' he assured Susan. 'Glad of your company.'

Grant began to talk about Antarctica. 'This'll be my fifth trip.' They sat at his feet as he reminisced...

Cliff-like icebergs, some the size of small countries, sailing sedately west. Mini bergs, craggy and sapphire-blue, which crackle. Water so cold the fish are equipped with their own anti-freeze - 'but hot enough, in one volcanic spot, to blister a ship's paint'. Air of such crystal purity that distant mountains seem a short walk away. Albatrosses, awe-inspiring as angels, circumnavigating the world. And leopard seals more vicious than you'd believe. Yet singing appears to soothe them, and shouting should scare them off. 'But don't think you can outpace 'em on snow. I've tried.' He rolled down his sock, exposing an old scar.

Neither Susan nor Gary showed any inclination to move. Grant, however, had to. He stood up. 'Oh, and you'll love the penguins. Unfortunately so do the leopard seals.'

At dinner, Darren's prize-money became the main issue. Despite amiable coaxing and cajoling, *no one* could persuade him to take it back. His wish was respected.

The bridge, an enclosed domain with its green-lit instruments, created a sense of calm. Philip Grant preferred night-watch. The men around him spoke seldom, sparingly. And he enjoyed being awake - like *Sea Shepherd* - while others slumbered, on board and on the invisible land sliding by. Yes, life was good...

Masterson crashed in, distraught. 'Curtis!' he panted. 'Over the side.'

'Christ! How long?'

'Three...four minutes.'

The ship was doing fifteen knots. Curtis might be a mile astern, Grant calculated. He strode to the chart table, fixed their exact position. 'Rouse the skipper.' His next order was to the helmsman: 'Hard a-port.'

Maintaining speed, *Sea Shepherd* came about and commenced retracing her course.

Loud-speakers in the crew's quarters blared MAN OVERBOARD. All hands rallied on the rails as look-outs. Preparations were made to lower lifeboats.

Alexander arrived, no less authoritative for his pyjamas and dressing-gown. He rapidly assessed the situation, then took Masterson aside. 'What the bloody hell happened?'

Sea Shepherd's powerful searchlight punctured the darkness, probing each wave. 'We'll be lucky to find 'im,' Grant murmured. 'Very lucky.'

Masterson explained to the captain. 'Curtis had asked to see me, late, and away from any eavesdroppers. He said he trusted me and would reveal new facts, vital facts. I went to his cabin. Foolishly I agreed to walk him round the deck. I had no idea, no reason to suspect...suicide. He jumped before I could stop him. I threw a lifebelt...'

Sea Shepherd completed her initial run, in vain. Curtis. Drowned? Drifting? Philip Grant plotted a fresh course, taking account of wind and currents, and turned the ship again.

Throughout the night *Sea Shepherd* traipsed to and fro - 'Dead Slow' - as if in memory of a man who must surely have perished.

At daybreak a sailor sighted a floating lifebelt. But that was all. The search was abandoned.

On deck, Captain Alexander and Johnny Masterson surveyed the spot where Curtis had plunged to oblivion. Alexander said, softly: 'He knew he couldn't win. One thing's clear - he wasn't gonna wait for the organization's revenge.'

When Susan and friends gathered at breakfast, they were aware of having slept badly but unaware of the drama in the dark. It was Ben Bellingham who told them about Curtis 'falling' overboard. A half-truth that would be expanded later.

Almost angrily Susan fumbled for her handkerchief. Why should she care? Then she noticed Darren's face and realised she was not the only one beset by inexplicable emotion. The conversations which followed were stilted, the silences full of unasked questions.

Meanwhile Alexander radioed London and wrote another bleak chapter in the ship's log.

With time to make up, *Sea Shepherd* quickened her pace - an increased tempo matched daily by those readying themselves for a frozen wilderness beyond the far horizon.

The students, lounging in the lecture hall, wished they were more than passive passengers. Little to do but read and re-read the background brochure issued by Ben. Norman seemed to have memorised nearly every word and was starting to sound as though he trekked regularly to the South Pole. Susan gave him a superior smile - *she'd* had the benefit of Philip Grant's personal experiences. And if Norman wanted to show off, why not?

'I say, let's have a quiz,' he suggested. The others played deaf. Norman, however, wouldn't be deterred. 'I'll start. Who is Emilio de Palma? Hey! Come on, you lot.'

Feigning indifference but unable to resist the challenge, Yves drawled: 'He was the first person born in Antarctica - in, er, 1977, I think.'

Norman: 'The year was 1978 and the place Esp...'

152

His words tailed off when the rest sang out mockingly: 'Esperanza base, Hope Bay.'

A sulky Norman blinked. 'Well, if you're going to be *stupid.'*

'OK, Prof,' Gary responded, 'answer this one. What's the largest penguin found in the Antarctic?'

Norman regained his cocksure manner. 'The emperor penguin, at $3^1/_4$ feet, two inches taller than the king penguin.'

'Wrong,' said Gary.

'I'm not!'

'Oh yes you are, Norman. You've forgotten that fossilised penguin scientists discovered, all $6^1/_2$ feet of it.'

'Trick question,' Norman fumed. 'Doesn't count.'

The quiz ground to a halt. But minds had been stimulated and, not surprisingly, general discussion developed (of *Sea Shepherd*'s polar assignment).

Their journey, which began on a grey English day nearly ten months ago, was drawing to a conclusion. And a climax? They were bound for the last frontier, a beautifully blank land where international specialists are studying the all-important mechanisms of nature. A peaceful continent 'belonging' to no one - though some nations had claimed a slice of the icing-covered cake, poised to exploit its rich ingredients. Already Antarctica is being soiled at the edges by pollution. Is this the future? Another man-made mess? Will maverick miners move in to wrench out coal and minerals? Will oil companies drill offshore until an inevitable spill spreads across the ocean?

Sometimes the teenagers lost touch with their ideals, their commitment to The Eden Mission, but not now.

In crisper air *Sea Shepherd* drove on past the tip of South America's tail. All anticipated a rough ride through Cape Horn with its notoriously wrathful winds; instead the ship met untroubled waters.

Escorted by albatrosses, she entered Drake Passage. Two days to go!

Onwards. Half-way. Temperatures plummeted - a chilly breath from the coming continent. They had reached Antarctica's threshold, the 'Polar Front'. Here, Atlantic and Southern Oceans dissolve into each other, causing an upsurge of plankton. Countless birds descend to feed and share the bounty with marine mammals.

It was Darren who spotted three or four butting whale snouts. Warmly wrapped, he and his fellow students eagerly noted every change in the seascape.

Glimpsing their first iceberg was a thrill. Captain Alexander felt differently about this mostly-submerged menace - too many vessels had been sunk. And bergs, melting faster below the surface than above, could roll over on top of you. Best to steer well clear.

Ahead, the waves subsided to become a flat white plain. Pack ice.

Crushing into it, *Sea Shepherd* soon found watery paths between the separate floes. Vanessa pointed to a chain of footprints, which Grant identified as penguin tracks. The furrows, though, were made by seals.

Gary and Susan shivered, feeling colder as a stiff breeze blew up. Everyone trooped inside to the comparative cosiness of the lecture hall, where observation continued from behind windows.

Dinner came and went. Time to think of bed. But, tired or not, who wanted to sleep while the sun shone as bright as ever on an ice-shimmering ocean?

10.00 p.m. Still broad daylight. Only at midnight, when *Sea Shepherd* was nearing land, did the sun dip, painting the peaks of piebald mountains in glorious reds and golds. Even then, it wasn't dark.

Two hours later, preceded by lavender shadows, the sun swiftly reappeared with flooding radiance.

Summer in Antarctica! Gary pitied his parents at home, enduring the drabness of an English winter.

Badgered by Maude Mimpriss, the students retired to their cabins. In the radio room, Ben notified scientific bases of *Sea Shepherd*'s presence. Most pleased to hear from him was the Greenpeace station on Ross Island.

Three Zodiacs, flat-bottomed landing-craft, ferried a party from the ship. Hard to tell who's who, Susan thought, eyeing her identically clad comrades. Scarlet expedition parkas, woolly hats, gloves, boots. And everybody's nose was greased against sunburn - mainly from snow-reflected light.

The leading Zodiac scrunched on to a gritty beach. Who'd be first ashore? Susan dutifully made way for Maude, but the teacher gave her gentle shove. She hopped forward.

Oddly, in the remotest and loneliest place on earth, they would meet many people: Russians, Poles, Chinese, Koreans, Chileans, Britons, Americans...a veritable United Nations of experts conducting varied research projects.

Several stations monitor the Ozone Hole, which opens each spring like a gigantic gash in Antarctica's sky.

At a British base, an affable meteorologist told his young guests: 'Between ten and thirty miles up, a gassy layer of ozone screens out the sun's harmful ultraviolet rays. So when we discovered the Hole, in 1984, it came as a global shock. Ozone is thinning everywhere, and doctors predict a steady rise in cancer and other serious diseases.'

Chemicals are the root cause of this damage, 'as I'm sure you know. Especially chlorofluorocarbons, chlorine-producing CFCs used in things like aerosols and refrigerators.'

Such chemicals disperse gradually, and most have yet to reach the ozone layer. Even if industry stops manufacturing them now - and it should - the depletion of ozone will continue for decades.

'Ultraviolet radiation is killing phytoplankton in the sea. These microscopic plants absorb CO_2, as do the rain forests. And, of course, CFCs and similar chemicals add considerably to the greenhouse effect.'

He folded his arms.

Yves asked: 'Why does the Hole open in spring and close in summer?'

The meteorologist leaned back. 'I'll *try* to put it simply. During Antarctica's bitter cold months of darkness, the chlorine I mentioned undergoes a peculiar change. When daylight returns, it triggers complex chemical reactions which result in the Ozone Hole. Later, as the atmosphere "thaws", those reactions cease and the Hole disappears.'

Yves nodded, half understanding. 'Exactly how safe is it outside?'

'Oh, safe enough - provided you take sensible precautions.'

After all they had heard, Yves was left wondering.

Monday, Tuesday, Wednesday: Skidoo (snowmobile) trips to collect fossils, and having to adapt to camping in tents with penguins as noisy neighbours.

Thursday: The students helped to launch weather balloons.

Friday: Weighed albatross chicks to assess growth.

Saturday: Out on the ice among snoring Weddell seals. No resistance offered by bulky bull when zoologists checked breathing rate, heartbeat, and attached a harness with electronic sensor to trace his movements.

Sunday: Finally, by boat to visit penguin colonies, called rookeries. Hundreds of thousands of braying birds - Adelies, gentoos, chinstraps.

'Poooh!' A fishy whiff hit Vanessa's nostrils. But the penguins *were* adorable. The chicks gulped shrimp-like krill as fast as their parents could catch and disgorge it. Again and again the adults dived for more. Many, though, dithered at the floe's edge...got ready to leap, then withdrew. Susan was puzzled.

Suddenly she understood. Right in front of the boat a penguin was struggling for survival, clamped by a leopard seal's jaws. Susan turned abruptly, burying her face in Gary's chest.

The marine biologist attempted to put matters into perspective: 'It's only doing what it was born to do.'

156

Nobody minded going back to base that day, certainly not Susan.

25 December. A morning lovelier than any they'd seen in Antarctica, a morning magically made for such an occasion. Aboard *Sea Shepherd* the mood among crew and passengers was as jolly as the multi-hued streamers that decorated corridors, dining-room, lecture hall and even the bridge. Though thoughts flew to families ten thousand miles away, the youngsters did not fret for home. This was their second home, their second family. And they were guaranteed a White Christmas!

The ship ghosted through drifting scenery.

She anchored off Deception Island, an active volcano with a sea-filled crater. Several Zodiacs skimmed shorewards. Soon after landing, Yves gave in to a mischievous impulse; but the snowball, dispatched with unintended force, missed Norman and caught Johnny Masterson smack on the ear. A delayed reaction before Johnny comically keeled over.

They all hiked to the crater...and looked down upon an eight-mile-wide lake, fed by the Southern Ocean. Then they descended inside, to the bottom of the crater, blinking in a humid haze. The black volcanic sand beneath their boots steamed like newly poured asphalt. And the green water beyond, bubbling with thermal springs, would be equally warm.

Gary, Susan and Yves stripped to their swimsuits, putting on canvas shoes, and scampered in.

Susan did an involuntary dance between hot and cold currents, trying to find just the right temperature.

Meanwhile, with the aid of thermometer, compass and other 'accessories', Norman was carrying out tests on everything in sight. 'Yep, that tallies.' He consulted his notes, aiming to impress Darren and Vanessa. But their sole interest was in the fun they were missing; both wished they'd been bolder and brought bathing-costumes. Norman again: 'Do you realise this volcano could erupt at any moment?' Vanessa: 'Thanks, Norman, you're such a comfort!'

157

A frogman emerged on to the sand and approached Johnny Masterson. Darren had noticed him earlier, exploring near *Sea Shepherd*. Johnny and the diver, 'an old chum', spoke briefly to each other.

Back on board for Christmas dinner. Turkey, plum pudding, crackers, paper hats, hugs, kisses, jokes - and a dignified toast to absent friends. Although she couldn't know it, Susan was not alone in including Leslie Curtis. Ben, temporarily free of worry and responsibility, made a superb gift-bearing Santa.

Sea Shepherd hooted farewell - to Deception Island and to Christmas.

Now they headed for a second British base, where the students would stay overnight. The ship dropped anchor and a boat was lowered. 'OK everybody?' Masterson started the motor. 'We're under way.'

For the teenagers, tomorrow held a full field schedule. No let up from work. But after a wonderful day like today, who could grumble?

14 Double-cross

B-O-O-O-O-O-O-O-O-M. A pulsating blast lifted the youngsters and their sleeping-bags off the floor.

Susan cried Gary's name.

All tried to clear their fuddled senses.

Norman talked excitedly: 'Deception Island! The volcano's going up! I knew it.'

BOOM...KABOOM...BOOM. Three more explosions sent tremors through the whole base, rattling walls and shattering glass.

Shouts, running feet.

Gary kicked aside the sleeping-bag and piled on polar gear over his night-clothes. The others dressed hurriedly, too.

Before long, unsupervised but following the general rush, they were outdoors.

Dank fog laced with sleet had shut down every view.

Norman and Susan intercepted one of the shadowy figures darting in and out of sight. The man, an engineer, leaned closer. 'Who's that?' Then he recognised them. 'Isn't Mr. Masterson with you?'

Norman: 'We haven't seen him since last night. He, er, went drinking with a friend. But what about the eruption?'

'Eruption?'

'Yeah, the volcano.' He gestured impatiently.

A fainter blast reached them.

When the engineer spoke again, his voice had changed. 'That's no volcano, I'm afraid. It's...your ship.'

159

'Liar!' Susan blurted. 'You've made a mistake. Not *Sea Shepherd*. It can't be true, can't be.'

The others echoed her desperate denial.

They surrounded the engineer. 'I'm sorry - but look, out there...'

The fog itself, orange-flecked, seemed to be aflame.

'Oh God!' Susan sobbed. 'What can we *dooo?*'

'Nothing.' The man peered over their heads. 'Go back inside and wait for Mr. Masterson. He's probably at the jetty - which is where I should be. Go inside, eh?'

But, of course, they didn't. Numbly, Gary leading, they stumbled to the shore. *Sea Shepherd* was engulfed in fire, a floating inferno that burnt away the cloud.

'Don't let them die,' Darren whispered. Yves heard him and said his own prayer.

At that instant, *Sea Shepherd* gave up the unequal fight. With an almost human moan she split amidships, bow and stern moving apart.

Regal even in ruin, her voyaging done, she peacefully went under.

Vanessa screamed. 'All drowned!'

But in the light of blazing oil on the water, Gary could make out familiar shapes. Small craft, fleeing. Two, three, five...

The first Zodiac landed, its passengers dishevelled and disorientated. 'Maude!' Susan ran forward and embraced the trembling teacher. And *there* was dear old Peter Stokes. And Geoffrey Baggalley.

One by one the boats came in, materialising out of a white-grey swirl. Above, a helicopter hovered.

The base was filling up fast. Priorities: medical treatment, blankets and plenty of hot drinks.

Captain James Alexander, gaunt and sunken eyed, waited for the last stragglers to assemble before conducting a roll-call. Most accounted for. Seven missing. Five crew, Senior Laboratory Scientist Cairns - and Ben Bellingham.

'*Ben?*' Vanessa swayed dizzily, but Yves caught her. Maude Mimpriss took over.

160

Feeling sick himself, Yves turned away and stood beside a desolate Norman to hear Captain Alexander say: 'The helicopter's still searching. There's still time. Don't give up hope.'

They *wanted* to believe him.

Sea Shepherd's chief engineer succumbed to rage. 'Cowards! Murdering bloody cowards!'

Alexander: 'The bomb, Chief. Planted underwater?'

'Yeah. I'd bet on it - Christ, the hull cracked like an eggshell.'

Susan's mind flipped. The ship gone...Ben gone...and now bombs. Too much to grasp, too much to bear.

Darren, however, was thinking about yesterday's occurrence on Deception Island.

Philip Grant joined them. Alexander unfolded a piece of paper, the message he and Grant received via the ship's radio less than an hour ago: ALEXANDER, YOU'RE A FOOL. YOU CHOSE TO IGNORE PREVIOUS WARNINGS. YOU ARE RESPONSIBLE FOR THE CONSEQUENCES - SEA SHEPHERD IS DOOMED. IMPOSSIBLE TO TAKE EVASIVE ACTION. THERE IS A BOMB ON BOARD. YOU'VE 20 MINUTES TO ABANDON SHIP. OR, IF YOU WISH TO DEFY US YET AGAIN, STAY PUT AND GO DOWN WITH IT...19 MINUTES...

GARSTON

Alexander stuffed the paper in his pocket. 'Nineteen minutes, Phil, not even that. I tried to get everyone off...'

'Don't blame yourself. If you do, you *are* a fool. No better skipper has ever sailed, or ever will sail.' The captain perked up a little. 'By the way,' Grant added, 'have you seen Masterson?'

'Good point. He was around earlier.'

As Vanessa reappeared, pale but self-possessed, Alexander's attention shifted to the students. 'Phil, perhaps you'd take our young friends somewhere quieter? And thanks.'

Grant found an unoccupied room. 'You won't be left alone for long.' He returned to the crowded lounge.

Susan fussed over Vanessa, but soon both were in tears. The

161

boys conferred miserably. Only Darren remained separate, plagued by thoughts he'd rather not utter. An underwater bomb, a frogman swimming by *Sea Shepherd,* the same diver who'd surfaced in the volcano's crater - any connection? If so...

The door slowly opened and Johnny Masterson entered.

'Johnny!' A relieved-sounding Vanessa.

For a moment he seemed to stiffen, as though startled.

She came nearer. 'Isn't it *terrible?*'

He nodded gravely.

Gary and Norman began quizzing him about Ben's chances. But before Johnny could respond, a stubble-chinned man, panting, stuck his head round the door. 'Ten-fifteen minutes, Garston, and the 'copter's ours.' Then he caught sight of the teenagers. 'Ah - you've got company. I'll push off.'

'Do that.'

Garston? Susan stared at Gary. Had she heard correctly? A hush, profound and intensifying. Who was this Garston?

Darren knew.

He remembered what the rest had forgotten: ROD GARSTON, printed in capitals, in Curtis's black book. Could he be sure Masterson and Garston were one? Yes...the facts drove Darren to an inescapable conclusion. Johnny Masterson, their trusted protector, was a fraud, a dirty double-crosser.

Darren sprang across the room. 'Get him! Garston - in the book! He's killed Ben!'

Bemused, not yet understanding, Gary, Yves and Norman hesitated. But the casual blow that winded Darren dispelled doubt.

They pitched in, Susan and Vanessa too. A melee of arms, legs, fists.

Garston grunted and, with a sudden surge of strength, heaved himself free of the attacking pack.

He drew a gun. 'Keep back!'

Darren was rubbing his stomach. 'Pity your frogman chum didn't blow himself up with that bomb.'

Garston jerked the automatic. 'In the corner, all of you!'

At first Susan did not obey. Part of her, against reason, clung to a shared past. 'Oh Johnny...'

Darren intervened sharply: 'Don't call 'im that.'

Garston looked almost uncomfortable under Susan's steady blue gaze. 'In the corner, I said!'

She retreated. 'You must really hate us. But you saved me from the Sea World kidnappers. Why?'

Holding the pistol on them, he uncovered his watch.

'Why?' Susan persisted.

Unexpectedly Garston gave her an answer. 'It was meant to scare Alexander off home. And even if it didn't, we knew it would establish my character. It was a set-up. Satisfied?'

Susan was lost for words, not so Gary. Recent events took on a new significance. 'God, I've just thought...Leslie Curtis didn't fall overboard, didn't jump either. You pushed him!'

Vanessa gasped. Yves wished the Christmas snowball he'd hurled had contained a rock.

No comment from Garston, who referred again to his watch.

Pressing their luck, the students discussed him with obvious contempt. Norman: 'Maybe *he's* the saboteur, eh Darren?' 'Very likely. And he let Curtis take the rap.' 'Shhh!' Gary whispered. 'Somebody's coming.'

Garston moved swiftly as the handle twisted. The door opened, concealing Garston behind it.

Geoffrey Baggalley strode in. 'Behaving yourselves?' His hearty manner softened before their strained faces. 'Try not to worry - things'll work out...'

He would have continued but for a hard prod in the back.

Meanwhile, bound for base, the helicopter banked steeply, its rescue mission completed. Not a total failure. Behind the pilot a medical orderly squatted by four blanketed forms - two dead, two alive.

Groaning, one of the survivors sat up and demanded to use the radio. The orderly restrained him gently. 'Relax and count your blessings.' He focused on the two fatalities, prey to the freezing

163

ocean. 'Could easily have been you.' But Ben Bellingham felt no gratitude, not yet, only an urgent need to contact Alexander. 'I must use the radio. Now!'

Ashore, Philip Grant called Captain Alexander to the radio. 'Listen to this.' Amid a commotion Ben's voice came over the receiver loud and clear. An astonished Alexander. 'Well, I'll be...' But his good cheer was brief, his greeting brushed aside by brusque inquiries. 'Is Masterson within earshot? Are the youngsters safe?'

Anxiously Ben waited, willing the right replies. Then: 'Jim... Masterson is an infiltrator from the organization...'

'A what?' Alexander pounded the desk. 'J-e-s-u-s!'

Bellingham: 'Jim...Jim. Are you still there?'

'Yeah, go on.'

'OK. Don't tangle with him - he's armed. We've gotta play it cagey. He thinks I'm dead, so let's keep it that way.'

Stretchered from the helicopter, Ben lay motionless beneath a blanket until - in a small office - he arose to shake Alexander's hand. Elsewhere, following strict orders, Grant and several other officers had to locate Masterson - no more.

Bellingham read the bomb warning, twice; Alexander pressed him for his part of the story. It proved an extraordinary account, which commenced after the Christmas celebrations aboard *Sea Shepherd*.

A problem involving revised schedules had led Ben to the captain's cabin. There, however, he had encountered not Alexander but Johnny Masterson, riffling through a stack of official documents. 'He was as surprised as I was, Jim. Why wasn't he at the base? He said he'd come back for some gear. Which didn't explain what he was doing in your cabin. I questioned him, civilly, in case you'd given him permission. He stalled. By now I was prepared for anything - except the gun.'

Forced along corridors at pistol-point, Ben had wound up in the deserted ship's laboratory. A crack on the head put paid to his protests. When he regained consciousness, bound and gagged, he heard lab scientist Frederick Cairns talking to his pampered fish.

164

Cairns untied him, and broke news of the bomb, the countdown well advanced. 'He gave me the *only* inflatable jacket.' It was just then that the bomb went off.

'Freddie staggered backwards. Water gushed from everywhere. The whole lab started to break up. I saw an oxygen cylinder working loose from the rack. I yelled, but it was too late. I couldn't get to him, Jim - there was nothing I could do.'

Somehow Ben had reached the steadily submerging deck, his last recollection.

'I tell you, Jim, I owe my life to poor Freddie.'

Alexander exhaled heavily. He paused, a mark of respect.

'Ben...what the hell was Masterson after?'

'Curtis's book. Have you got it?'

The captain glowered. 'No.'

Throughout this period, with a rifle issued by Base Commander Trent, Philip Grant and station personnel hunted high and low, in and around the complex.

A quick look into the students' room. No sign of Masterson. Grant asked: 'Where's Baggalley?' 'He's gone to the lavatory,' Yves lied. Grant nodded, closing the door. Garston had kept the gun on Baggalley.

Captain Alexander compiled a list of the deceased - five, including Cairns. Next, another grim duty. He picked up a phone, called London and reported to Conservation Committee chairman Sir Charles Fotheringay. Appalled beyond words, Sir Charles took several moments to respond. 'Masterson's clean, I guarantee it. We're talking about two different people...They *must* have used their own man!' Signing off, he vowed to trace the real Johnny.

Alexander prowled the office. 'So Masterson isn't Masterson. The stink gets worse.'

A pencil snapped between Bellingham's fingers. 'An impostor! Yes...of course...and Curtis found out who the impostor was and what he was up to. It's starting to fit together.'

'I'm not with you, Ben.'

'Look, we've been thinking of separate individuals: Johnny

165

Masterson and Rod Garston. We were duped. It's Garston... masquerading as Masterson!'

Piece by piece, Bellingham attempted to put the puzzle in place. What was Garston's role? To abort The Eden Mission. Also to spy on Curtis, a valuable agent but - perhaps - dangerously disloyal to the organization. 'Garston needed proof, and we provided it. The book alone was enough to seal Leslie Curtis's fate. But when he discovered Masterson's true identity...he had to be eliminated.'

Alexander: 'I suppose, in a way, Curtis unwittingly bought us time. The bastards couldn't have destroyed *Sea Shepherd* before they'd sorted out the Curtis affair. Ironic, really.'

Commander Trent knocked and entered to update Alexander and Bellingham on developments at the base. The helicopter had been grounded and was under surveillance. Trent asked: 'Your shipwrecker, Masterson, was he operating solo?' The captain considered: 'We've no reason to believe otherwise.' 'Then the back-up team is here on the base.' 'Team?' 'Afraid so. Two or three, I'd guess. I'll root 'em out.'

As Commander Trent left, he indicated the walkie-talkies. 'Stay in touch.'

Geoffrey Baggalley was doing what he could to lift the teenagers' morale. 'I'll never live it down - teacher stands in corner with pupils. And on my birthday, too!' Susan's own birthday memories were evoked. 'Many happy returns!'

Garston gripped the pistol tighter, frustrated, confined like those he must keep captive. At last his unshaven accomplice arrived. 'Trent's put the 'copter off limits. We're stranded!' Sneering, Garston raised the automatic. 'Who's gonna argue with this? Come when you hear the chopper's engine.' He glanced at the figures in the corner as though they were complete strangers. 'Watch them. Use your gun if you have to.'

Garston slipped from the room, towards a delayed getaway.

Only now did Darren recognise the man who had taken over as their jailer. Though he'd swapped wet-suit and flippers for polar parka and pistol, he was unmistakable: the diver. Darren taunted him. Anticipating retaliation, Baggalley tried to impose calm; but Darren grew bolder by the second.

Before Baggalley could stop him, he had stepped away from his friends and was advancing on the seated guard. 'Gonna shoot me, are you? You haven't got the guts. Not as easy as planting bombs, is it?'

Susan called out to him, but he dismissed her plea as he dismissed the loaded gun. 'Pull the trigger. Go ahead!'

The guard stood and aimed at the boy's head.

Darren thought of his father, of Curtis, of untold jungle fears, of choking guilt, of the person he once was...

'Go on. Do it!'

Terrified, Susan and Vanessa closed their eyes. Yves too.

The gun was beginning to shake.

'Go on. Shoot!'

Gary and Norman took a pace forward, Baggalley blocked them. 'Darren, shut up! He doesn't know what he's saying.'

Lowering the automatic, the man backed off, feeling for the door handle behind him. He withdrew further, half out of the room... and into Bellingham's bone-crushing bear-hug.

They rocked. Ben, red faced: 'W-h-e-r-e's Garston?'

Zip! A bullet splintered the floor. Baggalley hollered: 'He's heading for the helicopter!' Bellingham squeezed still harder. The pistol finally fell from a hand too feeble to hold it.

Alexander and Trent, soon there with reinforcements, required little briefing. Trent grabbed a walkie-talkie. 'He's on his way, Grant.'

The diver was carted off for questioning.

Darren approached Alexander. 'Captain, you'd better have this.' Gary goggled. 'The book! How did you...?' All went quiet. 'I picked his pocket. During the fight.' Then, almost apologetically, Darren added: 'I nearly didn't. It's the first time I've had to *force* myself to steal. I'm...I'm not a thief any more.'

The captain accepted the book. Darren looked up - and was the surprised recipient of a smart salute.

Alexander turned to address Bellingham. But he was gone, and so was the gun.

At Trent's suggestion Baggalley led the students back to the lounge, where they'd probably be safest. Darren would long cherish the captain's tribute. However, Geoffrey Baggalley expressed his views in a different manner. He admired Darren's courage, he couldn't deny that. *But playing games with a gunman...*

Susan gave Darren a smacking kiss.

Under interrogation, at which Alexander was present, the diver proved stubbornly uncommunicative. Trent both appealed and threatened in an attempt to loosen the conspirator's tongue. No breakthrough.

Ben Bellingham trod lightly, with a stealth acquired from years of stalking wild animals. He had needed no weapon then. Releasing the automatic's safety-catch, he eased round a corner. Garston had passed this way. A sprawled body marked the trail. The man was dead, a broken neck. Ben weighed the pistol in his palm.

Creeping along, he came upon a second casualty - groggy but able to stand.

Through a window, Philip Grant's task force kept up observation on the helicopter and the guards posted by it. One spoke into a walkie-talkie; the other, carrying the only rifle besides that in Grant's charge, stared about him. *When* would Garston make his move?

Garston - nearby, nearer than any imagined - could also see the guards. And, from an adjacent room, he could hear Grant speaking with colleagues.

Coolly Garston calculated a risk. Instinct guided him into the corridor. He was making his move.

Booting open the door, he shouted: 'Harris!' Grant levelled the rifle in Garston's direction...to find he himself was being targeted. Stalemate. But Harris, producing a pistol, tipped the balance. Grant had no option. Bitter, he surrendered the rifle to a person who, seconds earlier, had seemed as honest an ally as any.

Garston advanced menacingly on Grant. 'Do exactly as I say. Your men, out there, tell them the hunt's over. Tell them you've got me where you want me - all locked up.' He tapped the gun under Grant's chin.

Grant deliberately dropped the walkie-talkie. 'Forget it.'

'Wise up, Phil. Gary and Susan would like you to...and Vanessa, Yves, Norman and Darren. Nice kids.'

Harris: 'Craig's not with the kids. Trent's got him.'

Grant: 'Not quite going according to plan, is it?'

Garston: 'That's too bad.' Viciously he floored Grant, the pistol butt striking his jaw. Garston stooped for the walkie-talkie and thrust it forward. 'Get up and get talking!'

Grant stayed down. Garston kicked him. 'Get up!' But still he wouldn't.

It was Harris's turn to apply pressure. He picked on someone he'd known and worked with for many months, first slapping, then punching.

Garston stood over Grant. 'Harris doesn't know when to stop... Well?'

Wiping his mouth on a blood-spattered sleeve, Grant rose painfully. He contacted the unsuspecting helicopter guards.

As the two trooped into the room, they were seized and roughly disarmed. All prisoners were told to lie face down. 'No, Grant,' said Garston, 'not you.'

Harris and Garston pocketed their automatics and smashed every walkie-talkie. Now, with rifles at point-blank range, they shoved Philip Grant in front of them. A hostage.

From where he crouched, Bellingham had a clear view of the helicopter. He frowned. It was unattended. Did this mean Garston had been caught?

Muffled voices, away to his right, coming closer. Tense, ultra-cautious, he slipped into a doorway. He saw Alexander and Trent. They had hastened to investigate the walkie-talkie blackout, but didn't get that far. Unarmed, they were at Garston's mercy. Garston ordered: 'Face the wall and put your hands up! Keep perfectly still.' Grant winced as Harris clubbed both of them. 'Sleep well!' Harris sneered.

Ben silently withdrew from the doorway, taking his chance to stay one step ahead.

Outside, the air was crisp, sun-bright, with not a shred of fog. Philip Grant might have savoured Antarctic summer on top form. But, hobbling through snow, goaded and jabbed by a pair of thugs, he could contemplate nothing except his plight.

Pitiless, Garston growled: 'Faster!'

They reached the helicopter. Garston clambered in, stowing the rifle, and sat at the controls. Harris boarded next, an arm crooked round Grant's throat.

Garston pushed a button. Overhead the rotor blades stirred, whisked and whipped. Harris released his hold. 'Bye-bye, sucker!' Grant fell to his knees and, fearing a farewell bullet, started to crawl away.

Garston scanned the instrument panel. A-OK. Ready for take off.

'You're not going anywhere...cut the engine!' Behind him: a voice from the past, a dead man's voice. 'Drop your weapons!'

Garston felt a pistol digging into his cheek. 'Bellingham?'

Recklessly Harris fired off two shots; snow spurted around Grant. Ben reacted fast, but not before Harris had fired a third shot. Grant ceased crawling.

Bellingham clumped Harris, who tumbled unconscious from the cockpit. An action that left Ben vulnerable.

Spinning in his seat, automatic aimed, Garston clicked his fingers. 'Your gun!...C'mon!'

Bellingham passed it to him.

Garston: 'You've got more lives than a cat. If we weren't on opposite sides... You'd have made a fine partner. I like you, like your style. I'm gonna give you a break. Get out and keep moving.'

However, Ben didn't shift. 'It's over, don't you know that? You can't win, nor can the organization you kill for. Curtis's book will blow your sick and evil world apart.'

Garston smirked. 'You can't prove a thing without it.' He patted his breast-pocket, fumbled, searched another pocket.

170

'Lost something?' Bellingham's tone stoked Garston's growing fury.

'Give me the book!'

'*I* haven't got it. You're a bungler, Garston...Ugh!' The pistol rammed his ribs.

'Empty 'em, Bellingham! Your luck just ran out.'

A zip on Ben's parka jammed. He tugged repeatedly, but it wouldn't budge. Garston, his patience spent, tore at the clothing...

Ben struck. Both hands grabbed Garston's wrist, wrenching his gun-arm upwards. Off balance, Garston clawed Bellingham's face and fought to retain possession of the pistol. They wrestled wildly, banging back and forth in the cramped cockpit.

Locked together they plunged outside. They rolled in the snow, intent on the quivering gun. Advantage swung one way, then the other. Until...the pistol flew from Garston's grasp.

Bellingham was up and scrambling for the pistol. But Garston caught and tripped him. Spread-eagled, his fingers inches from the gun, Ben saw Garston snatch it.

There would be no reprieve, no last words, no crowing speech. Garston pointed the pistol.

Defying authority, Gary and Darren charged pell-mell into the open.

The sound of a single shot reverberated.

A score of witnesses - including Alexander, Trent and the students - stared in stunned disbelief. Disbelief deepened at fate unfolding before their eyes. Garston began to reel like a drunk. *Crack!* The fatal shot. Clutching bloody wounds, Garston collapsed. The bullets had come from a gun fired by First Officer Philip Grant.

Ben knelt to examine the still form of an enemy. Turning him over, he loosened the red-wet shirt and felt for a pulse that was no longer there.

Rod Garston was dead.

15 Round-up

And so ended one chapter in The Eden Mission story, a story that will continue as long as ecologists have a task to perform. Hope did not sink with *Sea Shepherd*. Instead her loss doubled determination among campaigners and drew new recruits to the conservation cause. Today, *Sea Shepherd II* plies the oceans, commanded by veteran James Alexander.

Philip Grant is sorely missed, invalided out of active service. Forever imprinted upon Ben Bellingham's mind will be Grant's courage in inching critically wounded through the snow to reach and use Harris's gun.

On the very day Rod Garston was buried, a solemn Sir Charles Fotheringay phoned from London to solve the Masterson riddle: Johnny had been murdered, his papers and identity stolen.

Craig and Harris had revealed the organization's audacious scheme to invade Antarctica and capitalise on the reserves of gold, platinum and uranium.

By then the students and teachers were back in England. Sighs, sometimes tears, had accompanied their parting from Ben and so many other comrades. The Greenpeace vessel *Gondwana* had carried them to Chile, where they boarded an aircraft for the flight home...sweet home!

As months passed, investigations based on Leslie Curtis's book resulted in the blackest future for all trapped between its covers. Law-enforcement agencies swooped on the organization's operations in Europe, America, Asia, Africa. Police raids ranged from Anilux headquarters in Hamburg to Colombia's jungle drug factories.

The Director, however, is still at large and rumours persist that *he* is the corrupt genius behind a revived organization. Nameless, elusive, a master manipulator, he made Maximilian Kruger a scapegoat - 'arranging' his arrest as the man who had authorised *Sea Shepherd*'s destruction. Kruger, believing arch-rival Art Benton to be responsible for this plot, incriminated him. Benton has sworn revenge...when both are free.

The youngsters, as promised, have kept in touch. Yves now lives in France, where Vanessa visits him every summer. Norman is studying to become a specialist on global population and associated problems. Gary and Susan, of course, see each other often. She particularly values a memento Darren gave her, something he'd detached from a ship's trunk barely 48 hours after embarking, a brass plaque engraved *m.v. Sea Shepherd*.

News of the teachers is relayed by Maude Mimpriss, who writes twice a year to her former pupils and takes more than a professional interest in them.

The six won't forget their unique adventure, their modest contribution to a worldwide crusade for change.

Thanks mainly to conservationists, concern about the living planet has never been greater. 'Green' issues are fashionable. Governments and industry pledge reform to protect our environment. But, while man-made catastrophes recur and fresh follies loom, The Eden Mission cannot rest.

The David Bellamy Solar Study Centre Appeal

The Centre for Alternative Technology, Machynlleth, Wales was established in 1975 and has become one of Europe's leading centres demonstrating sustainable technology and ways of life. The difference between CAT and other centres is that technical progress is presented through a practical, hands-on environment built to encourage public participation.

The new Solar Study Centre is a state-of-the-art building project providing superb facilities for CAT's educational courses, conferences and seminars, for both residential and day visitors. The Centre will use modern technology to make maximum use of passive solar heating and generate electricity from the sun, so achieving major energy and CO_2 savings with minimal environmental impact.

It will also provide a working display of these technologies for the visiting public and help to publicise, throughout Europe, the potential for sustainable building design and solar energy.

The Centre will feature unusual environmentally friendly characteristics such as central heating supplied by a woodchip boiler, toilets flushed by rainwater and electricity derived from renewable resources. Winter heating bills will be reduced by 87%. Green timber, from local sources, is used in the construction of the Centre for minimal ecological impact, and an innovative Reed Bed Sewage System will dispose of waste naturally.

The David Bellamy Appeal for the completion of the Solar Study Centre is helping to establish a fitting mile-stone for the 20th anniversary of The Centre for Alternative Technology.

Useful addresses

Wildlife Trusts
Witham Park
Waterside South
Lincoln
LN5 7JR

Greenpeace
Canonbury Villas
London
NWI 2PN

Friends of the Earth
26 Underwood Street
London
N1 7JQ

National Trust
36 Queen Anne's Gate
London
SW1H 9AS

Marine Conservation Society
9 Gloucester Road
Ross-on-Wye
Herefordshire
HR9 5BU

Born Free Foundation
Coldharbour
Dorking
Surrey
RH5 6HA

Respect for Animals
PO Box 500
Nottingham
NG1 3AS

Royal Botanic Gardens
Kew
Richmond
Surrey

London Ecology Centre
45 Shelton Street
London
SW2H 9HJ

Scott Polar Research Institute
University of Cambridge
Lensfield Road
Cambridge
CB2 1ER

RSPB
The Lodge
Sandy
Bedfordshire
SG19 2DL

World Wide Fund for Nature
Panda House
Weyside Park
Catteshall Lane
Godalming
Surrey
GU7 1XR

RSPCA
Causeway
Horsham
West Sussex
RH12 1HG

**Whale and Dolphin
Conservation Society**
Alexander House
James Street West
Bath
Avon
BA1 2BT

**Centre for Alternative
Technology**
Machynlleth
Powys
Wales
SY20 9AZ

Ark Environmental Foundation
Room 643
Linen Hall
162 Regent Street
London
W1R 5TB

Animal Rehabilitation Centre
The Cottage
Hough-on-the-Hill
Nr. Grantham
Lincolnshire
NG32 2BB

**Woods Hole Oceanographic
Institution**
Woods Hole
Massachusetts
02543
USA